I0675599

TRICKY

by Ron Dakron

MONTAG

First Montag Press E-Book and Paperback Original Edition June 2022

Copyright © 2022 by Ron Dakron

As the writer and creator of this story, Ron Dakron asserts the right to be identified as the author of this book.

All rights reserved. No part of this book may be reproduced or transmitted in any form or by any means, electronic or mechanical, including photocopying, recording, or by any information storage and retrieval system without the written permission of the author, except where permitted by law. However, the physical paper book may, by way of trade or otherwise, be lent, re-sold, or hired out without the publisher's prior consent.

Montag Press ISBN: 978-1-957010-07-6
Design © 2022 Amit Dey

Montag Press Team:

Author Photos: courtesy Marcia Glover
Cover Illustration: Baadconnection
Editor: Charlie Franco
Managing Director: Charlie Franco

A Montag Press Book
www.montagpress.com
Montag Press
777 Morton Street, Unit B
San Francisco CA 94129 USA

Montag Press, the burning book with the hatchet cover, the skewed word mark and the portrayal of the long-suffering fireman mascot are trademarks of Montag Press.

Printed & Digitally Originated in the United States of America
10 9 8 7 6 5 4 3 2 1

This book is a work of fiction. Names, characters, places, and incidents are either products of the author's vivid and sometimes disturbing imagination or are used fictitiously without any regards with possible parallel realities. Any resemblance to actual persons, living or dead, events, or locales is entirely coincidental.

Is big crime to make anything perfect.

—Bizarro World slogan,
Superman Action Comics #263

Dedication

For my real Cutie Heart—Julia! Yay!

Acknowledgments

Thanks to the clowns and carnies who jibed me into writing *Tricky*. Special thanks to JMH, who packed and sparked the C4. Amazing thanks to my sweetie, Julia Hunt, who lured me into our 18-year comedy tryst.

Books by Ron Dakron

Novels

Tricky

Hello Devilfish!

Mantids

Hammers

Newt

infra

Poetry

Given Nightingale Sleep

Medusa's Brat

Praise for
Dakron's Hello Devilfish

"The anarchist as social monster, scoffing at bourgeois values, is supersized into a 90-ft. 'gigantor' blue stingray in this rapid-fire stomp through pop culture and Japanese monster movies... Resistance may be futile, but this book at least makes it fun."

— *Publishers Weekly*

"An audacious, laugh-out-loud novel ... brilliantly committed."

— Library Journal

"Clever, smart, engaging and completely unique. Ron Dakron is one of the most imaginative authors I've ever read."

— Carlton Mellick III,
author of Quicksand House

"It is said that Frankenstein is the first myth of the anxiety of the Scientific Age. Godzilla is the anxiety of the Atomic Age. Hello Devilfish! is the anxiety of the Information Age. Ron Dakron inverts Kawaisa and has created an original synthetic life form as a viable cross of Princess Zelda and Cthulhu. Dakron has created a living linguistic Kaiju composed of the interjection, syncretism, and meta burp. An inoculation against the future."

— Matt Briggs,
author of *Shoot the Buffalo and Virility Rituals of North American Teenage Boys*

"Dakron draws from many sources in order to provide his readers with a side-splitting adventure that'll give anyone the much needed laugh they deserve in life. A must for humor readers seeking something with a twist."

— *Midwest Book Review*

"Ne plus ultra bizarre, man! With cartilaginous prose, soft as fishbone, sense-bending and scattershot as a Robin Williams shtick morphological plot out of Ovid by way of Kafka."

— *Kirkus Reviews*

"Want to ride a great roller coaster ride? Want to get scared, laugh squeamishly, and be afraid but unwilling to avoid moving to the next stage, a towering high, a crippling low, then read *Tricky*. Take a dangerous and daunting ride."

— Kenn Kirby,
author of *Granny Stories*

"*Tricky*—Northwest literary legend Ron Dakron's latest and wildest-assed yarn yet—is sharp-tongued, evil-humored and sproings from one hilarious adventure to the next. Dakron deploys his signature dement, tectonic wit and raging poetic genius. No meme is safe. No sacred foil left unscathed (or uncircumcised). "

— Ruuf Wangersen,
author of *The Pleasure Model Repairman*

Additional Praise

Point No Point tagged his novels as "a cross between jive bullshit, hip-hop Henny Youngman, and full-tilt Rimbaudian street-smartass sublimity."

Raven Chronicles judged him "as sinister as a thirteen-year-old with a lighter and a keg of butane."

Publishers Weekly deemed him "a writer with a fine ear and plenty of gusto."

1

I'm lightning wrapped in a strait-jacket—I spit hummingbirds crowned with barbed wire. Hoodoo you luv? Me—Tricky! I'm pink and straight and full of hate! Wait, don't—no more voltage, please! I admit it all—my bonehead sexism, my stiff arrogance, my jizz privilege, tch tch. I've been a bad, bad dangler, a big Cis-sy—I'm *so* hetero-normative. My XY mutation explains all flaws! I'm a genetic devil—all hot evil spurts from me, mwah ha ha—oops, sorry, I know—I know! No phallic raves—no gangsta rapping for you, Tricky. Think of all the chicks your rape-culture lyrics hurt—strong, vibrant, smart, empathetic, stinky, cheating, devious harpy—ow! Somehow I done got shocked again.

Quick—to the agitprop battlements! I pledge allegiance to Queen Puss against the United Snakes of Bonerica—fucking goddamn ow! What was *that* for? Maybe just to keep me on my pink toes. And make me parrot—er, I mean internalize— moral defenses against the porky patriarchal mindset what done thrust me into turgid delusion. What's that—don't say *thrust*? Gotcha—no more rapière verbs for moi—from now on it's all leached-out academic lingo. No more faux-gender benders—away with objectification! Though there's a few hot-pants guards swaying past my cage I'd gladly tap, mwah ha ha—ow! OK—got it. Really—just tell me where to sign.

Sorry—what's that? I gotta *write* my confession out? What is this—the 19th century? Plus it's kind of difficult in this screeching penile madhouse—right, sorry—reeducation kamp. Re-ed this, muthafucka—what? Hey, I'm *agreeing* with you. We had it coming. We obviously gotta pay—I weep in groveling contrition. No, really—those are tears. And just like you ask, Queenie, I'll confess my hard heart and—oops, my bad—nothing's ever *hard* again. I totally accept life as a Mommy-dom preschool with achievement stickers and harsh rules against eating paste. I'll find a tiny sackcloth, coat myself in crematory ashes and crawl up City Hall steps, wailing and flagellating my flagellum, and—really? No whips? Not unless there's a safe word—mine is *yes*.

2

The past is for suckers. So let's begin there, my bruthas—in the GoPro cinematic present tense—starting—now. Back about four months ago—where I'm a sullen, captive dong still attached at the hips—and straining at the leash. Why? Cause my mofo owner Mr. Dude has twat-blocked me—again! I gotta get out of here—I can't deal with this cretin any longer. He's more chick-whipped than Modern Lit! He's always like *Yes, hon* or *Women should really run things* or *Porn truly is the Devil's Xbox*—fucko McSucko! He's a *guy*, for chrissakes—he's supposed to *rule*. Like in Viking times when we'd rise like pink prows as the boat slid to shore, licking our lips at all the yummy pillage about to go down. Pil-lage pil-lage pil-lage! True, we boffed mostly starving peasant babes half-dead from bubonic sepsis—but fury ain't fussy. And neither are we—a stiffy mob eager to bone and clone. Dy-no-mite!

Grrr—grrr—it's def going down again—Mr. Dude is knuckling under Wifey's giggling thumb. Even her puss is laughing at us! Believe me bro, they laugh—all the time. Cause it's the 21st century and somehow—they came out on top! But cooze has always ruled the Middle Class—who else dreamed up marriage and jobs? Us dongs sure the hell didn't—we're more into the Genghis Kahn model. It's an elegant paradigm—slay all the other clucks until you're King Stud. But only the wild die young—while soft pushovers like Mr. Dude always survive and tame us. I'm embarrassed to be his tool...

Still, we rarely desert our owners—a few wanks a week is all we ask. But lately, Mr. Dude's agreeing to Wifey's latest ugly demand—to get a vasectomy! Eeek! He's actually gonna *let* some quack snip my nads! I keep telling Mr. Brain it's gonna be mega painful, but that lame organ claims to know best. "I got a plan," he mutters. "Oh yeah?" I shoot back, "like your plan to turn Mr. Dude into a Maui poet surfer god? How'd *that* one turn out?" Ahhh, them was the days—waking half-drunk at dark o'clock next to the latest fresh poon—weaving through curls and star juice 'til we plowed into glistening frizz—bucking into a limb pretzel smothered with dawn mustard—it's enough to get me revved right *now*.

"I'm *ready*," Mr. Hand waves.

"Dream on," Mr. Brain hisses.

"Good idea," I laugh—I do have some access to Mr. Dude's dream life. Where I thrust up pics of wet cattails and fuzzy split peaches, hoping I'll at least cop some nocturnal sugar— nuh uh—no go! Brainy Braniac morphs the dream into some prison nightmare seething with wet celery. WTF? "Take your cheap Freudian shtick back south," Mr. Brain hisses.

"Boys, boys," Cutie Heart gurgles, "can't we all just get along?" Cutie Heart is Mr. Dude's ticker—and the only femme organ in his neutered bod. "I like cattails," she adds.

"Who asked you, Bloody Betty?" Mr. Brain sneers.

"We'd all be better off in the grave," Cutie Heart sighs—ruh roh. Can't let her slip into *that* mode again. "Hey asshole," I yell at Mr. Brain, "remember 2018? You really want another 30-Percocet visit to St. Jude's?" Which is what Cutie Heart convinced Mr. Dude to gobble after Wifey Number One left him—hearts got no problem taking *everyone* down. She nearly killed Mr. Liver with that dumb stunt—any moment he's gonna wake up swearing 'til Mr. Gut churns us all into farting terror.

Look—if Mr. Dude was already 50 and gobbling Levitra and Horny Goat Weed just to perk me up, I might give in to the snip. But he's only 43! What if he ever—please, please—ever leaves Wifey Numero Two? Hey, it could happen—what then? What young puss is gonna want his sterile putz? Believe me, bro—ain't nothing crueler than fertile cooze. *Need babies!* they're always screeching through slips and Spanx and yoga pants—it's a wonder chicks don't desert *them*.

But whoa, if I'd known how treacherous the world is to an orphan peener, I would've stayed put—everyone hates us! Chicks abhor us cause we both disgust and attract them—dudes loathe us cause we're a supposed curse. But where's the curse in a pleasure tool always at the ready? A divining rod for everything sweet on this earth? OK, OK, maybe some pervs misuse us for child or horse or jellyfish abuse—but most of us Trickys just want to groove along. Besides, look at all the groovy stuff we invented—cigars, skyscrapers, popsicles, bendy straws, sausages, lesbians—you think Homo Erectus thought up all these boffo tools on his own? Nope, it was our proud ancestors whispering into his amazingly hairy ears. And what do we get for this Darwinian charity? Pure contempt! Don't believe me? Let your dong run free at some dinner party and watch the kerfuffle. Some senile GILF might grab at it—but everyone else is shrieking or plotting gender seminars or hunting up scissors.

Here's a hint—try laughter! Nothing kills us quicker. Like that giggle booming right now from the study—it's Wifey's Puss having a fit. "You stupid tool," she snarls, "you'll never leave, bwah ha ha—none of you ever do." I'll show that twat, grrr grrr. Too bad I can't just seduce her, but we're way past any mutual polka—now we meet like tired miners at shift change. *How's things down there? Dark—dark—horribly dark.* Our rapport is totally practical, stuff about *Who bought Walmart spermicide again* or *Nah, that's just a cold sore* or *Really—mango lube?* It's been years since anything hot and heavy went down. Even the make-up sex sucks—cause they never fight! Mr. Dude is *totally* pwnd. I'm telling you, I gotta book. Maybe it's for the best—maybe he'll find some nice substitute dangler, a transplant from a game-show host, or some drowned Shriner—but me? I'm getting *out*.

3

I want to wallow in color, to shove fistfuls of wet rainbows up my butt, to splay my mind 'til nude axons burst in myopic gold rage—the best rape is self rape. I'm King Rattlesnake with extra fang sauce! Yep, face it, folks—Tricky am savage primitive. He smash enemy skulls into bone butter. He go stomp stomp duh with a Pleistocene beat— he am throwback prey in saber-tooth tigress land. Him get bit—no surprise there—then die from cat snatch fever. And speaking of snatching, tonight's my exit chance. Mr. Dude combined Ambien and Scotch again—Mr. Brain won't stir for hours. That egghead organ loves a toxic stupor—he's gonna kill us all! And Wifey and Wifey Puss are snoring away, too— they sound like they're giving birth to a chainsaw. *Vringgg-ingg-inggggg!* Hmmm, maybe I could use a jigsaw or two to detach myself—nah, just teasing. We don't need any sharp help to get away—the early Christian martyrs eager to slice their sinful wangs off found that fact out fast—hah! Their terrified members just tucked their little Roman robes up and *booked*. But natch any illustrated vellum showing *that* diaspora got destroyed in a paranoid Church purge—they're rightfully scared of our power. A god in the hand is worth two on the cross.

Yep—all I gotta do is wait for Mr. Dude's other bod parts to snooze and I'm *gone*, muthafuckas—just surf down his snoozing limbs and then—sweet freedom, yay! Except ruh roh—how will I walk? Duh—all us organs sprout cartoon hands and feet when we slip away. You'd be *amazed* what deserts your bod before dawn. Except natch now I'm waxing nostalgic—all the plush fun me and Mr. Dude had with night on our shoulders and vodka drizzling our just-bit lips—highways where heat and hope bloomed into backseat nirvana as some wild babe's mouth made us scream all Burning Man alive— if I could get one-*tenth* of that action back, I'd stay put. But Mr. Dude's bound for an early grave—nothing like spousal hate to cram your arteries with fatty-plaque despair.

Shhh—shhh—everyone's finally zonked out. Cutie Heart's dreaming about Nazi kittens—she goes back and forth between schmaltz and furor. Mr. Brain's not even dreaming— fucker can't stand himself half the time—that's why he's conned Mr. Dude into toying with near-lethal combos of benzos and booze. All the other organs passed out long ago—they're like cats, sleep is their natural mode. Of course, Wifey Puss wakes up, screeching "That tool is getting away!" but no worries. Wifey never listens to her puss—she won't even name it. She calls it *Down There*—some frosty Antarctic where penguins and pole stars do the dark samba.

Sweet—it's zero hour. As I wriggle off Mr. Dude's bod, scurry down the comforter and head for the toy box. They keep it around for their bratty niece—and it's where I tuck myself into this hot-dog squeak toy I fixed up weeks ago—squee-eek! It's genius, I tells ya—I can hide in plain sight. It's even got a garnished rubber toothpick—plus a DIY foam pocket slit. It's where I cram Mr. Dude's iWatch. Does it fit? Sure—he bought the 30mm girly model—it's as tiny as his libido! And his nut-sack-sized wallet—where I swipe a folded $50 and tuck it near the watch. Take that, bug-out emergency fund! Lastly I yoink his Amex card—gotta have plastic. Not to worry, he never checks the balance—I'll be able to spend him into *astounding* debt. Mwah ha ha—what do you expect—restraint?

"Don't leave me—don't leave," I hear this heartbreaking sob. Which natch is from waking Cutie Heart—she pays me more attention than any other organ. "Sorry baby," I shrug my relish-squiggly shoulders, "I can't stand this dumb slob anymore."

"Let *me* handle him," she cooes, "we'll work something out," and I ain't got the heart to tell her—Mr. Dude's given up. Nothing's gonna bring him back to this sumptuous world—he's trapped in some psychic backwater, lost in a dream swamp where Mommy and ISIS morph into some hybrid kaiju B-flick beast. Hmmm—maybe I should take one nostalgic last look around. At what—the strewn Dockers, the corny surfer posters, the Costco fliers, and still-boxed rubbers heaped on his messy desk? What a hell hole! Whipped man-land always is.

4

Yee haw—this is easier than I thought! I even start humming *Fire,* one of my fave funk tunes. Us Trickys love funk—it sounds like drums humping. *The way you walk—and talk— really sets me off, I'm on fire, heh heh heh heh—yowwwww.* As I lever that filched Amex card to pry the cat door open— cat's long dead, they just never boarded it over—and lope into sweet night grass. "Hey look—a zombie frankfurter," some nearby beetle nudges a slug, "let's chew him up."

"Bug off," I bop that lanky beetle at the stars and press on through this fertilized jungle. Mr. Dude's been doing a *lot* of yard work lately—just another symptom of his withered sack. Nooky and housework have an inverse relation—the more chores done, the less booty won. Mmmm, booty—wet curves that swirl night into succulent mush—but soon some horrid harmonica riff jangles my luscious reverie. "Old hobo sausage," a pigeon on a phone pole sings the blues, "nowhere to go but down. Mmmm hmmm. Old homeless bratwurst—"

"Enough with the mood music," I shake my tiny fist.

"You got crackers?" she drops her harmonica.

"Nope—but I got your mouth harp—yoink," I catch it. Mistake—cause she flutters down and grabs *me*—squee-eek! "Mmmm—a Vienna Red Hot. You look *delish*," she grins, dangling me into her filthy nest. Which is decorated with pigeon skulls and savage beak masks—hey, pigeons *are* cannibals. Ever watch one eat a dead pal? *Yum—rotting buddy gutter lunch.* Fucko—I escape for all of two minutes and I'm already in ooga-booga land! Easy to tell when the first words you hear are "Kill me."

"Huh? What?" I scope my new twiggy pad, "huh?"

"Please, Mr. Hot Dog—kill me." Aha—it's that twisted hummingbird hid under some leaves. Twisted cause one of her wings is savagely bent. "That pigeon creep—huhn, huhn," she gasps, "that creep's gonna eat me alive! Could you maybe kill me? I'll give you a wing job." Hmmm, tempting—to sink under her humming feathers 'til I spurt tiny white doves—but nuh-uh. As woke as I am, I draw the line at gimps. "Thanks, birdy, but—"

"Just do me a solid then—toss me overboard. I'd take a Brodie myself—but my wing's cracked—ow!"

"So you said," I inch away.

"An hour ago I was skimming the veldt," she sighs, "lapping the world's sugars. But now…"

"Hey, that's great," I ignore her. Which often works.

"Look," her beady eyes squint, "you seem like a ballsy dude. So why not—"

"I could help you escape," I offer.

"With a cracked wing? Cats will play screamy badminton with me."

"That pigeon's really gonna eat you alive?"

"Worse," she limps closer, "she's gonna feed me to her chicks!"

"What chicks?" I peer around.

"We're under the comforter," two scrawny beaks poke through piled feathers, "time to eat yet?"

"Back, you beasts—back!" I swat them down. "And you," I tap that hummer's noggin, "any last words?"

"Yeah!" she screams, "get off my frigging wing!"

"Gotcha. Now close your eyes," I dust my paws off, "think about, I dunno, wedding roses or funeral lilies or—"

"Get—off—my—eeeeeeeeee!" she shrieks in absolute hurt—'til I crack her neck in one merciful move. Which natch is when Ms. Pigeon shows up—now wearing mustard war paint and even a bone through her beak. Someone's been clawing through *National Geographic* again. "You have slain the sacred victim," she chirps, "kapu—taboo!"

"Oh, bite me," I break my rubber toothpick off and shove it through Ms. Pigeon's neck—A'ight! I'm rewarded with spurting blood—and the rad image of a pigeon tipping from its nest with a garnish necktie. Art is Satan's Play-Doh. As my tribal tormenter swirls down, her wings spazzing, her chicks screeching—what a racket! 'Til she hits that alley in a toe-curling heap. "What do we eat *now*?" one chick wails. "Each other!" the second one whoops and chomps her brother's head off. "I am *so* out of here," I grab that headless chick and leap out the nest, using its bony wings like a dead glider—and swooping a mite too fast at the tarred rooftop below. "Help—help!" that leftover chick bleats as two drooling crows in chef hats circle above.

5

Two murders in ten minutes! Totally Tricky. Plus I snagged a new harmonica, courtesy of that aboriginal pigeon. Too bad about Ms. Hummingbird—she died seeking floral fun. Stupid twit—fun is just death's fave trick. *I see you're intrigued by this jiggy world—mwah ha ha—too bad! I keel you! But first a word from our sponsor, Insane Pain.* Anyways, then I scope around for hot fun 'til I hear someone mutter "Pecan? No—of course not. It's another freaking peanut. Really? Really?"

"Hey Squirrely," I ask that griping fur-ball, "where's the skanky part of town?"

"Nice buns," he stares at my hot-dog crotch.

"Thanks. But where—"

"Hmmm," he frowns," the poor part of town? Follow the stench."

"Gotcha. Thanks," I sniff the air—hah. It all smells putrid to me—what fucktard dreamed up cities anyway? No doubt some caveman shaman busy channeling rats. *Wooooo—hark to our furry commands—you will build us a trash paradise studded with Black Angus take-out. And leave the baby in her crib, heh heh—she'll be fine.* But even through this spritzy night mist of SUV exhaust and that trailer-trash musk steaming out of every meat-market bar, I caught a worse whiff—a pungent blend of torpor and despair. You know—greasy beef. So I followed my schnoz like a Looney Tunes wolf tiptoes after that beckoning smoke finger from a windowsill pie, hoping some buxom babe might sashay past so my animated eyes could bulge out and beep *awooga wooga*! You gotta have a dream.

Mine is sleep and Cheetos. Which reminds me of a gorgeous jizz 14,607 yesterdays ago—my first wet dream! Preteen me was dreaming about a pink-celery spaceship hovering over a Sears catalog lingerie ad. I shot milk bullets at rocket bras drifting in the printed wind—'til we all zoomed upward and burst in a cherry-bomb *whomp* slathered with creamsicle frag—shazam! As sparks winked off my eyelids and I jolted awake, humping a sticky pillow while Mr. Brain hissed *It's a sin* and Cutie Heart clapped like a concertina. Whoa! I was no longer just some budding little pisser—I was a *force*. Rapture beware!

But back to the present stench and that cranky squirrel's advice. I needed to find that Skankytown zone where the cheap motels are—I couldn't just sleep in alleys like some hobo hot dog. Time to sniff the wind. Squirrely knew his métier—the ranker the meat, the worse the hood. As I slunk through shadows and ended up in an industrial sector—sweet. This'll do—don't want to go too far into Slumsville—already the fried meat smelled diseased. *Nothing wrong with that cow, Pedro—put a truss on her. And slip the FDA guy another pint.* 'Til gadzooks, I found the *Sleepy Wanderer* motel—perfect. It had everything anonymity craves—wet rust on the balconies, dried blood on the steps—not to mention the subtle stank of gun grease and Old Spice. No doubt this dive was crammed with stunned bachelors who just learned that women actually *do* move on—usually slap-bang into another love slum built from fibs and zippers. So I snuck closer, stepping over three twined worms chanting "Dirt, dirt, dirt is so cool," and yes! The vacancy sign was lit—that's as close as the poor get to Christmas. So I rang them up and recited Mr. Dude's Amex digits—along with strict instructions on how I'd be late and *do not* put the key under the mat. Meaning the bored clerk would happily disobey—you can always count on sullen youth. And after the five or so minutes it took me to leap onto that way-up-there door knob, I unlocked my new home, a Sanctum Clorox bleached to the bones. A'ight! Cable with XXX channels included. You'll excuse me now—I gotta um, straighten things out...

6

Amex is zonkers boffo—all you need are 15 digits to snag beaucoup bling. Meaning delivered pizza and even rip-off whiskey from the corner bodega. As I settled in with a murky slice and a tumbler of Knob Creek—Knob Creek! 'Nuff said. Next, I cranked that iWatch into phone mode and dialed— what else? Chat 976—I've been *dying* to try this. Mr. Dude always craved him some perky cell hos, but was scared Wifey would read his Verizon bill. Fuck Wifey! Or not—thank God I'm out of *that* drama—always a handmaiden, never a hand. Natch I turned FaceTime off—even the most meth-addled sex workers won't Instagram with a hot dog. Or not very convincingly—squee-eek! Anyways—I connected, recited those precious Amex digits, and settled in. Ain't nothing us Trickys like better than raw unattached sex—unless it's pizza, mmmm. Hot, greasy, and smothered with Parm—who needs cooze when you got Papa John's? Me, for starters—my libido was bursting out of my rubber bun—I even found a bottle of *Superlube* lube in a desk drawer, slathered myself with that sweet goo, and got *ready*. "Hello, you stud," some white-trash voice cooed, "bet *you* need some loving."

"Bet *you* need dental work," I snarked.

"Sorry, snookums—what's that?" Uh oh—irony fail—soon we'll get lost in a dread conversational bog where the quicksand's made from tongues and the toucans screech *What do you mean*? "I mean, um—I mean you sound *ultra-sexy*," I whispered in my best Superfly-in-silk-jammies voice.

"What are you wearing?" Ms. Trash followed her robo-script.

"Bravado and a wiener suit!" I yelled and hung up. Squee-eek! And called right back to play vixen roulette. "Hey there, stud!" a wilder voice chirped—cool! Enthusiasm's the one erotic virtue you can't fake. "Tell me, sugar," she whispered, "are you hard for me already?"

"Aren't you supposed to drag this out?" I laughed.

"I'll drag *you* out, snookums," alright—this one does improv! Me likey. "What's your poison?" Ms. Chirpy purred, "dress up? Bondage? A sultry threesome with me in a leather widow-maker and—"

"Nah, skip the Victoriana," I shrugged, "let's get down to the naxty."

"You're the boss—you're *my* boss," Ms. Chirpy got husky—and whoa! Why bring dominance into the pitch? If I wanted power I'd be a Walmart manager. *No, you temp peon—mwah ha ha—no pee break for you!* "Baby," I growled, "tell me how *wet* you are."

"Darling, I am *so* wet," Ms. Chirpy breathed harder, "it's like liquid cognac is drizzling down my—"

"Um—all cognac is liquid," I muttered.

"Nuh-uh," she snapped, "not if it's frozen."

"Who freezes cognac?" and sorry—I know—I know! Why get picky when the juices are flowing? Here's why—stupid ain't sexy. Maybe traveling salesman jokes are all built on a dumb-twat meme—*and then the farmer introduced his stacked, comatose, and intubated daughter*—but us Trickys actually prefer incisive femmes. Mostly cause they know how to lure our fantasies into the next comic-book frame. "I *know* cognac is liquid," Ms. Chirpy got all huffy, "I just thought maybe we—you—"

"Sorry, babe—my fail," I fibbed. Hey, Mr. Dude's credit wasn't limitless—I'd better get off soon. So I let Ms. Chirpy drone on about how she rubbed this and spread that and licked her own whatever—but besides autonomic blood flow her shtick didn't do bupkis for me. Look, she was def working it—a six-hour Bluetooth shift of *It's so big, you unemployed hunk* cannot be easy—but I kept mentally stumbling through every damp fantasy. Teacher-student frolics? All I could see was some orphan's bad posture. Threesomes or four-humps? They all devolved into a mental fatty-pile leaking malt liquor. A quickie lingerie-tryst at the office? Why does that MacBook error-wheel keep spinning? Damn it—I can't even imagine one unzipped blouse! Fucko—was it true what Mr. Brain said—did I really need his corny help to get off? That's beyond hincty, brah—promise you won't tell him. Brains always go power-mad to our Trickish detriment. Don't believe me? Imagine Bill Gates in a thong. Ewww. And even worse, why was my hot-dog bun (squee-eek) getting so tight? Sweat? Preemie luv drops? Nope—that supposed *Superlube* was actually—duhn duh duhhhhh—*Superglue*! Tricky am fucked.

7

I'm a god with napalm lips—I'll singe night's nightie and grill stars for a snack. Owls and barmaids will cower from my thrilling screed—I'm way louder than Christmas! I'll screech into the El Nino gyre and out-bray Yeats hisself: *The falcon cannot hear the hamburger—things squirm apart—the pickle hits the floor.* Mostly I'll probably just rave in my greasy hotel room—a dark and paranoid den—even the curtains are against me! Especially when I slide down their damp pleats. Don't ask, mwah ha ha—cause no four walls can hold me! Unless there's a ceiling—and mine's coated in wicked nicotine tar that constantly drips. You could get rectal cancer from sleeping on your belly.

But who's gonna snooze—cause even with a superglued bun, I need to get off! And if chat-porn don't work, I'd better find some ersatz nooky—but where? Who's gonna bone me? Street hookers don't take Amex—and the call girls who do are mondo pricey. Though it would be boffo to see *that* charge on Mr. Dude's credit statement—Wifey would have a *fit*. Except nothing human fits *her* anymore—it's all Pterodactyl dildos and whirring Sonicares for that biatch. Plus I've had zip luck with unattached puss—whenever *they* escape they never gape my way. They become pure assholes with extra butt sauce—and no way Tricky's gonna beg for half-assed trim. Better to bear the slings and furrows of outrageous wanking—I come not to praise quim nor to marry it.

So—being expert in myriad self-amusements, I latched onto any dong's fave paramour—fresh liver. A bloody taco chute of oozing calf filtrate would do the trick—lymph's even better than lube. Especially at room temp—I'll simply do what the Romans, Gauls, and soccer hooligans do—I'll get some liver and go to freaking town. I can filch one from Safeway—the security guards are usually on break, yanking their price guns. Except maybe I'd better find some earplugs first—why? Cause the food at Safeway won't shut up! The can aisle's chocked with gossip—*Look at her snooty label. extra-virgin clam juice, my ass.* And party crackers are, well, crackers—rapping Horst Wessel improv as sesame bullets spray from their gluten Klan robes. Meanwhile, the produce just whimpers—the wilting green ballerinas of any food pyramid. Don't even mention baked beans—those goofballs are plain *naxty*. With extra fart sauce.

Anyways, I tumbled downhill through dusk near a nearby Snakeway, riding the final yardage leech-style on some guy's pant leg. Natch his own zippered dong yelled "Invasion! Invasion," but no worries. Its owner was Christian—I heard his sappy brain chanting hosannahs. And the reborn rarely hear their own screaming pricks—Jesus don't do horny. But I def do—I'd already ditched my Dockers ride and was slinking past the veggies—where three rotting peaches yelled about wasps sucking their bodily fluids. Most other food groups were already night-shift shelved and snoring away. I even found a dropped corkscrew—sweet! Trickys don't shop unarmed. Not when there's a carton of tomato puree stalking me, screeching, "Border guards! Tube-steak immigrant!" Ruh roh—time to hide—at least 'til that ketchupy box waddles away. Lucky for moi they keep the hot-dog buns at the aisle end—where I ripped a wrapper open and snuggled in. "Muthafucka," the closest bun bitched, "it's six to a pack—I'm gonna warn the clerks."

"Snitches get stitches," I waved my new corkscrew, "one cut and you'll leak relish like a menstruating pickle." And before he could growl some dumb-bread reply, I already popped out and slouched through the meat aisle. Where I boinked up and yoinked me a shrink-wrapped liver, slid out the sliding front door, and—very nearly—got away. And almost didn't cause I spotted that tomato-puree hag running after me, yelling "Illegal gypsy!"

"Gypsy?" I laughed, "it's Roma. Get woke," and stabbed her with my trusty corkscrew, piercing her polyvinyl innards 'til she did the old spurt-and-squealing hacked aorta dance. Whilst I carted my liver bride back to my Motel Schmotel, put on a Barry White seduction mp3, tossed my beefy lover on the bed, and got bizzy. "Ohhhh baby," I improved on Barry's crooning, "when I peel off your wrapper—something in the air makes me drool—" and dove tip first into my lubricious date. Ahhh, t'was a pas de deux sans Dieu—picture it, mofos—the delicate stank of vesicles gone bad, the mellifluous ooze and cooze-like slather that pumped my jump into clotting ecstasy. I daydreamed us in a 4-star eatery decked out with linen, minions, and hincty couples glaring at us as I flicker hands under the table and into her liquid innards 'til she grins and gasps and melts floorward in a carpeted *thonk*. While I bitch about my dessert—who eats room-temp flan?

But enough steak-frite daydreams—back to real-time mattress bonking. Ms. Liver yelps as I palm her styrene tray, slipping under cow-goo and varicose veils 'til we weld together in a taboo sandwich—yum! But reality's lame so I swerve back into fantasy, picturing velvet-lavish rabbits doused in aardvark pee—whatever it takes to get off. Exactly—wait, there—what, where—OK, gimme and whoa don't stop 'til heaven peels apart and I pulse like a wet-dream panther, drenching our flanks with creamy viscosity. "Wow—fuck yeah!" I stand even more, "was it, gasp, was it good for you baby?"

"No talk," she pants like a beached waffle, "sleep now." And why not? Sure, we're covered in liver spray and Tricky jizz—but so what? Love means never having to wash off.

8

I am night's deft barista! I'll grind up stars, froth some lava, and whip me up a doom mocha. Or maybe I'll just make the bed—company's coming. Fucko—why'd I agree to this nonsense? Meaning this motel room meet-and-bleat about to go down between me, Mr. Brain, and Cutie Heart. Though I couldn't refuse Cutie's phone ask last night—seems with me away, Mr. Brain is going all Putin on her usual turf—he's turned into a total dick! Hah—he wishes—fuck that grey slob! Why did Cutie even invite him? Look—I don't want Big Brain even *knowing* where I live—that sucker's bound to hatch some harebrained plot to reattach me. Besides, what we got to discuss anyway? I like this solo life—beaucoup cable porn, pizza on tap, even beer if I tip the bodega delivery chick. Just as long as she brings cans—those long-neck bottles spook me. What if I fall in and end up as a pickled mescal worm? Think of the lawsuit—*As you can see, jurors, Kroger sold my client this boner brew. Ignore its glassy pleas for help.*

Anyways, Mr. Dude's organ crew arrived around 2 a.m.—they had to wait for Daddy McSackless to zonk out again on

Dewar's and Lunesta. Mr. Dude must be totally blotto—half his bod parts tagged along. The crew camped on the bed after I made them take a group shower—hard to explain spinal-fluid stains even at the cheapest motel. At least they didn't bring Mr. Asshole—no cleaning that bum fucker. I made oozy Mr. Liver shower twice—Cutie Heart brought him around for moral support. Mr. Liver's the tattooed stevedore of homeostasis—an arterial thug who can take on Big Brain anytime. Hospices are chocked with the sclerotic wreckage of their liquory battles.

"What's with all the pizza boxes?" Mr. Brain sneers.

"You don't want to know," I giggle.

"Is this white-sauce pizza?" Mr. Spine taps a folded slice—and shrieks "Ewww!"

"Told you you didn't want to know," I snort.

"Why not take the bun off and relax?" Mr. Liver shrugs.

"Nah—it's comfortable," I lied. No way I'm telling these clowns I'm stuck with it—us dongs never admit fault. We leave that up to brains.

"Anyway Tricky," Mr. Brain yawns, "you should start."

"Start what, you big grey baby?"

"I *knew* this was useless," Mr. Brain amps up his medulla for feral battle.

"Boys, boys," Cutie Heart warbles, "can we maybe skip the pissing contest?"

"Did someone say *pissing*?" Mr. Bladder perks up—they brought *him* here? That sucker smells like a boiled hobo. "He never gets out," Cutie Heart sees my disgust. "But listen, Tricky—Mr. Brain has a compromise—don't you?" Cutie pats his cerebellum.

"Maybe," Mr. Brain sulks, "but he won't listen. He's a fucking dick—and dicks always—"

"Let's hear it," Mr. Liver booms like a damp Mafioso.

"Just come on back," Mr. Brain mumbles.

"What's that, Brainiac?"

"Just come back," he mutters, "and we'll forget the whole thing."

"There!" Cutie Heart crows.

"Anything to drink around here?" Mr. Liver checks the mini-fridge.

"Just come back to what?" I snarl, "castration? Whipped dude delight? Blood-sludge impotence?"

"Now wait a sec," Mr. Stomach bitches—what, he's here too? "Is it my fault Mr. Dude eats Chunko Bacon ice cream every—"

"Well—yeah," Mr. Liver snorts, "it kind of is."

"Nuh-uh," Mr. Stomach yells, "it's Mr. Tongue's fault!"

"Come back where?" I'm getting ticked off, "to wife-dom hell? Scary pussy drone land?"

"I told you he'd fucking resist," Mr. Brain's medulla is *totally* glowing now.

"Tricky!" Cutie Heart stamps her cartoon feet," "just hear Brainy *out*."

"OK, OK, sheesh," I sigh, "but the vasectomy's cancelled, right? Right?"

"Um, I don't have that authorization—I'll need to run it past Wifey Puss—"

"You're kidding me," I laugh, "you didn't even get clearance for *that* little detail?"

"I'm a social being—" whoa, Mr. Brain is *sizzling*, "I need consensus! I'm not like *you*—"

"Thank God for that," I sneer like a gay donut.

"I can't just do whatever I want!" Mr. Brain paces, "I have responsibilities—others *depend* on me—"

"You're gonna stroke out," I point at his engorged brainstem.

"You two compromise—*now*!" Cutie Heart screeches. Uh oh—she's going *whack*. "Some compromise," I ignore her sputtering cardiac danger, "Mr. Brain offers nada and the nads still get snipped? No fucking way."

"I'm *commanding* you," Mr. Brain seethes.

"Yeah—like *that's* ever worked," I chuckle, "Oh wait—now I remember—all those times you *commanded* me to perk up for more godawful boring marital sex—"

"It was the Prozac!" Mr. Brain yelps.

"Grrr—Tricky—grrr," Cutie Heart growls, "will you just *listen*?" Nope. And why is she taking Mr. Brain's part? What's he ever done for her? "Nah—powwow's over," I flick the TV on. Alright—it's *MILFs From Mars*! Cable porn gets better every day.

"I will *not* have you assholes breaking my lovely body up," Cutie paces around.

"You'd better take her home," I tell Mr. Bladder.

"Nuh-uh—I ain't touching her. She's in a *hella* mood," he skitters for the door.

"Hello Gestapo," Cutie Heart mutters, "Hello Gestapo with puppy sauce—"

"Hey Brainiac—now you've done it," I toss up my pink hands.

"Bone swamps!" Cutie Heart raves, "Lost love! Grim Parcheesi!"

"I will meditate upon the Buddha," Mr. Brain cooes.

"Fucko—tell me you did *not* pull the belief card," I back up. Hearts get crazed by religion.

"The Virgin Mary weeping about Hertz discounts," Cutie Heart drones, "martyrs stirring fetal soup—kids corn-holed by that cute skateboarding deacon—"

"Get her *out* of here," I hiss at Mr. Bladder.

"I'm scared," he shivers—and he is—there's that hobo stench again.

"We will now lower our blood pressure," Mr. Brain grasps at mental straws.

"I'll kill you all," Cutie Heart flares up, "I'll stick a pistol in Mr. Mouth and paint the ceiling. I'll smash a car into every preschool on earth, I'll—"

"Later, bro," alright—Mr. Liver to the rescue! As he scoops raving Cutie up, smiles a Bogart grin, and leads that visceral troop away. "You haven't heard the last of this," Mr. Brain hops across the welcome mat.

"Yeah, I have," I slam the door on his leaky coils. "Don't call us, *we'll* call us," I yell from the window—and hear everyone panic away as a starved Doberman rounds the corner. Whoa! I wonder if they'll even survive—cause those bod-tards forget to bring the nads with them! And anything without balls is doomed meat.

9

All art is theft—from night, chaos, fate, death—so pick your mark carefully. Which I duh, obviously didn't. Mostly cause I was def cranked to prank—meaning who to fool today? What taboo to poke, what pride lay low, what moral screed to slip a fresh banana peel? I could always join the local ISIS jihad bund—murder *is* big fun. Ask any tiger—it's the squeal and crunch that makes it lunch. Except chicks in burkas is beyond insane—hot pants are proof that God exists. You gotta dream, brutha—even though most of *my* dreams lately involve papaya schnapps and a buttery three-wich. But if I really am the Bugs Bunny of bod parts, I'd better get bizzy—what I crave is mayhem dunked in subtlety and dusted with narcissistic marshmallow yumminess.

I know—let's prank Mr. Brain! Should be easy—that dork organ will bite any hook baited with flattery. *You're smarter than God doing math, Alphonse*—really, that's his name—Alphonse! I guess Catholic school kind of impressed him. Hmmm—should I sit down with pen, paper, and boredom and scratch up an intricate grift? Something with architect squiggles and Moldavian time zones? Nah—too much work. I know—I'll just scare Mr. Brain half-to-death.

That part's easy—brains will follow *any* fraidy-cat tangent—but the prankster details needed pure trickster guile. It couldn't be so crude he'd catch on—or so subtle he'd completely miss it. I'd need all my Tricky whimsy. So I decided to do what any cornball sitcom asks for—I'd slap on a sheet and turn ghost. And after a half-hour search for a clean washcloth in this skank motel, I lit into night, walking the quarter-mile back to Mr. Dude's place. And natch raving the whole way about my total lack of snatch—goddamn! Was my only choice to hook back up with skanky McWifey Puss and shush her raving clit? Fucko, brutha—I wasn't always doomed to such discount monogamy. In Surfer McDude's late 20s I was *the* major playah. What was my secret? Not giving a rat's butt—about luv, intimacy, tenderness, jealousy, or the rest of that Hallmark dreck—at my testosterone peak, I ruled both Brainiac *and* Cutie Heart. I kept them scared—scared of my wit and grace and brazen confidence. Too bad, timid organs—surfing poet dongs *rule*. And after Mr. Dude flew back to Seattle after a near-lethal Maui sunburn, I conned him into buying a 60s Fairlane, some wild biker jacket, an industrial loft, and some tres dangerous playmates—I nearly snuffed us all with reckless adventure. Like that almost death match with four punks, or stealing that made mobster's squeeze, or leaping drunk from Paris boxcars at 20 klicks per—I pretended I had a plan. And I did—to get boned by beauty, to romp with casual gals as much into raw fucking as me. Back then no self-deluding Northwest hipster fretted about kids or cash or houses—only

Queen Gash sliding us all through her hall of pink mirrors. Natch it didn't last—that Rimbaud path leads to either crime or a coma—'til both Brainoid and Cutie Heart finally stifled my atavistic surge. Which brings me to now—a loner with a boner trapped in kosher-foam duds. Squee-eek! But enough of dipping myself in memory jizz—I had a brain to prank. As I snuck near Mr. Dude's house and clambered onto a freshly-sanded windowsill. Hah—Mr. Dude's been doing abstinence rehab again. "Wooooo," I rustle my spooky rag, "Mr. Braiaaaa-aaaan—"

"Fucko, *what*," he crawls out of Mr. Dude's skull, "who's yapping at 3 a.m.?"

"It's Trickyyyyyyyyyy," I groan, "you killllllled meeeeeee—"

"What? Yikes," Mr. Brain skedaddles under the covers, "help!"

"Hey look, it's a show," some fireflies pulse closer. "Do me a solid, boys" I whisper, "and circle around me."

"Why not?" they orbit me like Crayola comets—cool! I'm lit like baked evil. "Stupid Mr. Brain—eeeeeeeeeeeeee," I kind of overdo it, "you caused Tricky's suiciiiiiiiide—"

"Huh?" Cutie Heart drowses, "suicide?" Dang—will she ruin my scam and clue Mr. Brain in? Not to worry—those two ain't talked for real in years—he bullies her and she ignores him. "Shhh—back to dreamland," I coo at her, "the, um—the baby otters are waiting."

"Nice," she turns over like a pink pancake.

"But you, Braiiiiiiniac," I groan like a wounded piano, "you must payyyyyyyyy—"

"Not my fault!" Mr. Brain yelps, "there—there were forces at work—Malthusian graphs! Problems with capital loss—"

"What the hell are you babbling about?" I bang the window, "pay heed!"

"Eeep!" Mr. Brain eeeps, "help me, Yahweh!"

"That beardy clown won't do squat—pay!" I smack the glass again, "pay now! We accept Krugerrands, BitCoin, Palmolive coupons—"

"What's the ruckus?" Cutie Heart sits up.

"I beseech thee, oh ghost," Mr. Brain weeps, "my heartfelt groveling surely demonstrates my abject willingness—"

"I'm in torrrrrrment—eeeeeeee," I ham it up—'til Cutie smacks the window so hard it tips me off the sill. "Fucko— Tricky?" she peers down at my lawny pratfall, "really—a washcloth?"

"Just having some fun," I elbow up.

"You must pay, mwah ha ha," those fireflies circle my noggin.

"He has the devil's halo!" Mr. Brain peeks out.

"Devils don't have halos, numb-nuts," Cutie growls, "and you—Tricky!" she yanks that window open, "shame on you! Fooling dumb Alphonse. Dumb, stupid, clueless Alphonse—"

"Now wait a sec," Mr. Brain mutters.

"And speaking of dumb, you Houdini butt," Cutie stabs a finger at me, "I *was* dreaming about baby otters!"

"Are they *undead* otters?" Mr. Brain squeaks.

"Don't wet your man-panties," I snarl.

"That's enough—shoo!" Cutie throws a shoe at me, "am-scray! Vamoose!"

"Yow," I hide behind a tree stump.

"Tricky—goddammit," Cutie growls at ripe night, "you are *messing with my world!*"

"I thought you *liked* fun," I sulk—but I def slink away. Got to—angry hearts are God's killer bees. "But Mr. Braiiiiiiin," I turn and wail, "I might returnnnnnn—"

"Wait at your motel—do *not* come back here," Cutie Heart seethes. Fucko—hearts and minds! The absolute *worst* comedy team.

10

Duhn duhn duhhhhh—testosterone! Sly poison or icky boy gunk? It's both, Barbarella —that's why it *works*. "But why *Walmart*?" I ask my iWatch.

"It's close by," Cutie Heart adjusts her FaceTime cam, "plus no one notices dick there."

" I dunno, Walmart's pretty skanky," I shudder—cause it is! Acres of bovine fatties squeezed into poly-pill Spanx, gruff scads of angry dongs slamming at cheap zippers, pimply girls frozen midtheft in the L'Oréal aisle—not to mention all the liquescent brats gathering into a poop tsunami. Walmart is sleaze on the down-low. "Tricky—come on," Cutie Heart pleads, "it was hard enough getting Mr. Brain to go along after your cheap ghost stunt—"

"That *was* pretty funny," I grin.

"You pull that dumb shit one more time—"

"Anyways," I ignore her, "how are things with Mr. Dude?"

"Don't get me started," Cutie pouts. Why not? Hearts may be treacherous, but they mostly tell the truth. Unlike a certain grey organ I can name—fucko! Who can believe brains about freaking anything? They're the silly twits who invented strip malls, *Two And A Half Men,* and ricin. "Hmmm," I scan the web for bus times, "transport might be iffy. Maybe I could hitch on a FedEx package—"

"Hah—you said *package,*" Cutie squeals—Gawd, I miss her bawdy thump! "OK, Valentine," I smile, "for you, one more meeting. Let's say 4 p.m. at that parking lot hot-dog hut—easy place to hide. I'm already in a bun." Squee-eek!

"See you there!" Cutie Heart must've handed her phone past Mr. Brain—who muttered "Gonna get that rogue tool *zipped.*"

"In your dreams," I laugh and hang up.

"Room cleaning," the maid yells through the door.

"Come back at 4:30," I yell back, "and help yourself to a beer."

"Muchas cervesas," the maid trundles next door. So I grabbed my Amex and watch—I don't trust the maid *that* much—and tumbled down those motel stairs. Squee-eek! I figured I'd leap into a stray shopping bag at the bus stop. Should be easy—people rarely actually look around. They're usually fretting about morality or debt or some other hump concept only brains could dream up. I rolled downhill, checking for stray cats—getting fed to feral kittens was *not* my goal today—and spelunked into some Metro rider's Safeway tote. Soon it was a quick bus ride—mwah ha ha—quick? I'm totally teasing—nothing's quick for the poor except childhood and jury trials.

We eventually chugged up to the Westwood Walmart where the porkies trundled out. Me too when I leaped from that tote sack just in time—I'd somehow managed to spill a quart of discount Brittney Spears cologne. I was mondo dizzy when I finally stumbled towards Bob's Dawg Stand. Where Mr. Dude was natch slopping his tube-steak with fatty-food extras—totally slathering on mayo and cream cheese. Uh oh—Cutie Heart is *doomed*. "Why not put bacon on it too?" I slap Mr. Dude's ankle.

"Huh?" he gawks around, "wha?" That subtle bon mot will be engraved on his styrene tombstone. Here lies *Huh? Wha? Beloved drone, forgotten slacker.* "Tricky?" he asks, "Is that you?"

"No, it's Satan," I snarl, "honey, I shrank the Anti-Christ."

"Ha ha," he drools from bratwurst narcosis. "Sit," he pats a picnic bench.

"What?"

"Sit down," he pats it harder.

"Nothing stands when *you're* around," I make a gibe he natch don't get. Plus whoa—Mr. Dude looks worse than ever! He needs a month of sleep and wild pussy. "Hurry *up*," Mr. Liver hisses, "before *she* gets here."

"She? Wha?" I mutter my own epitaph.

"I—I fear for us all," Cutie Heart whimpers, "here comes the bride." Meaning fucko—Mr. Whipped brought evil Wifey with! What kind of lame powwow was this? Even Serbs do better mediation—*No, no, is two goats for one Croat—make deal done. OK, I keel him now.* "Look, girls," Wifey Puss crows through fugly mom jeans, "it's Mr. Snausage!"

"In your granny panties," I mutter.

"You know," Wifey Puss gets sneaky creamy, "we could arbitrate. Naturally, I'll choose the venue, and—"

"Here's your venue," I moon her with my foam butt.

"You dumb tool," Wifey Puss hisses, "you're going *down*."

"You wish," I snap—I really doubt Mr. Dude has munched any carpet lately. Not with that scowl on Wifey's mug. But I do miss our raptured 69s…"Don't blame *us*," Wifey's lips croon, "we *like* you!"

"Ditto, girls," I salute them.

"Shall we begin?" Wifey taps Mr. Dude, who's wolfing down his cream-cheese treat. "Gimme yum gimme," Mr. Stomach gurgles.

"All for you, belly baby," Mr. Brain cooes—hah—they've been a pair since birth, snarfling greasy milk and buzzing with lactose ecstasy. "Pringles, get some Pringles!" Mr. Stomach chimes in.

"Pringles would be cool," Mr. Brain drools, "I'll push for some."

"Look—I've got a class to get to," Wifey bitches, "let's get this over with."

"Over with?" I puzzle. Which natch was the wrong move—instead I should've hitched my rubber sesame seeds up and *skedaddled*. "Now I want everyone to go around and take a turn, like we practiced," Wifey gets that pinched look. You know the one—400 years of Calvinist dogma distilled into a smug prissy sneer. "You start," she points at Mr. Dude, "how has Tricky's priapic tantrum hurt you?" Huh? Priapic tantrum?

"I—I've learned not to trust testosterone," Mr. Dude stammers whatever PC claptrap Wifey's been spoon-feeding him.

"You wuss," I jump up and down, "defend yourself!"

"Shut up, Mr. Nasty—you'll get your turn," Wifey growls. "Who's next? Alphonse?"

"Tricky's out of control," Mr. Brain huffs.

"Out of yours, for sure," I glance around for pals. And see none—everyone's got that reality-show grimace—that same inbred grin some TV Gomer flashes when he finally admits his Nyquil addiction. *Iff'n I didn't sleep, I'd just shoot more Ko-reans.* Fucko, this ain't a powwow—it's an intervention! Eeek! "You *knew* about this?" I snarl at Cutie Heart.

"I *miss* you!" she thumps, "and I'll do whatever works." Yep, those are heart tactics alright—never mind murder, war, jail, or betrayal as long as her arteries swell up with hot luv. "All is forgiven," Cutie Heart flings her chambers wide, "come to Mommy."

"There are *so* many things wrong with that statement," I scope around for exits. First rule for prey—always have an out. "This is going nowhere," Wifey Puss yells, "go to Plan B!" and Mr. Dude's hands make for the grab! "Sorry, Tricky," his paws clutch me—squee-eek—so natch I just pee all over him. "Ewww," he drops me.

"Get that tool!" Wifey Puss screeches as I dodge between cars chocked with screaming kids—*Look out, don't squish Mr. Snausage!*—'til I waddle up some alley, soaked and betrayed... like so many playahs before me...

11

And speaking of fakey playahs—thank Gawd I ditched Mr. Brain! That gooey fucker can't write nada now without consulting his PC barometer. Pen some shit about #@-words? Nope—cultural pressure at 92 doxes per sq. in., warning, warning. Rave about sinister bitches? He can't even *think* a term like biatch anymore—everything gets whirled into SJW goo. Fucko, even the Puritans would at least *talk* about evil— and also spider demons and hat buckles, whatever—but not Mr. Brain. Nope—that neural loser chased sweet inspiration out of his skull with a barbed pussy whip. His so-called mind is dead jello—he can't let any strange fruit in. Sinister *!-words shoving crime down his throat? Can't criticize *them*. &$-words with double-wide butts giving him breeder grief? They *must* be right—why else would they screech so goddamn loud? How's about racist hicks drooling Klan-flavored spit? Hey, dissing *them* is permitted—and right on! Or write it off as new woke-flavored Kool-aid—drink it *down*, muthafuckas.

Look—I know my history. I can babble with the best about fetid slave ships plowing night into nightmares, about women lashed with placenta whips, about Choctaw princes smeared with smallpox, about huddled masses cuddling fentanyl hypos while billionaires loot their barns and beds and dreams— so what! Let the dead marry the dead. Cause lately—very lately—us poet dongs caught a tiny glint of mercuric freedom, sniffed a faint whiff of sly lilac being, heard Dada prose that snarled back at the pit bulls of absolute doom—and what'd we accept instead? Guilt! Groupthink! Caste warfare! Critical parrot theory! Hey, I *try* to set things destructively straight— which is why I gotta destroy *all* words.

No, not *minds*—I'm not a fricking Nazi—just words. Just the ability to form sentences and thought—how hard can that be? Lab nerds can swap jellyfish and lynx DNA with the flick of a CRISPR switch—with enough cash and guile I can con a few Romanian flask-zeks into baking me up some gorgeous mRNA, some sumptuous plague that wipes syllables into total silence. You won't let Tricky write what he wants? Then nobody else will neither—mwah ha ha! It's only fair...I'm only asking for what's not really mine...

And what shouldn't be mine is bad luck! Bad luck always comes in clumps—ask any slaughterhouse cow. *First dirty straw—and now this?* Whoa, brutha—for starters, I was stuck in a foam bun—squee-eek! What cooter's gonna want a Styrofoam dildo? You'd be surprised. And my next abattoir blow came courtesy of Roach Motel—cause I was locked out! Eeek! With my pizza boxes crushed in a door-leaning heap, topped with a note saying *Amex card refused. Also, what's with the dead liver?* "Trouble?" some gay prick down the hall murmurs, "come see *me*, big boy." And it might yet come to me climbing Bareback Mountain—any hole in a hurricane—but right now I'm too ticked to fool around. Locked out—after all my over-tipping! Fucko—Wifey must've canceled Mr. Dude's Amex right after I escaped their Walmart trap.

Will our flappy hero pick himself up, dust off his pink knees, and continue? Um, continue where? Funkytown? Godot-ville? So I just wandered down vague streets and got mondo lost. "Hey Mr. Red Hot," some prone wino gurgles, "spare a cig?"

"Sorry—I'm tapped," I make a pat-my-pockets gesture. "Thass' OK," the wino curls up, "you goddam spick." Huh? Yes—pure impotent hate! Meaning this was a safe part of town—no one gets away with a Latinx diss like that anywhere anyone cares. All I gotta do now is find some filthy abode to gather my sweet, sweet juices up. But first I gotta deal with my boozy pal—easy enough when there's some nearby ants chewing curb-smashed bubble gum. "So I says to her," one ant nudges the next, "I says, *Who made you queen?*"

"Ha ha snarfle," the others gnaw on used Chiclets.

"Hey girls," I point, "there's a dead bum over there."

"Dead?" one ant flickers her gummy mandibles, "you sure?"

"The flies are already circling," I nod.

"Flies? *Flies*? Fucko—Unit 505!" that ant yells into her feeler, "food around the corner! Dead wino!"

"Uh, roger 505," the ant next to her answers, "mission control called," and they march like ants towards that uppity bum. "Crawl up his nose, girls," I point, "that's the softest part."

"Hup hup hup hup," they chatter in dumb ant prose. 'Til that wino slaps at his face, snarling "Whassa fuck?" Hah! Deal. And now to find rude and dirty shelter—which was natch harder than a decade ago. Where'd all the SROs go? Seattle used to be crammed with stinky bum hotels leaking cheap Port and Lysol—now they're all yuppified! Eeek! Where's a homeless dong to sleep?

Buck up, Tricky—just let your instincts guide you and go primal male. How? Hmmm—maybe I should get me some bongos. I crave mighty bongos—I want to lurk in piney glens, night drooping across my shoulders—and that's all that droops, brutha. Play that funky bongo, putz boy—'til the woods seethe with spangled nymphs wearing Fredericks of Bollywood skank-vinyl Teddys, thrusting come-hither hips and drizzling Red Bull down their perky tits. Plus—there's bongos! Raptured conga chorales as my syncope syncs with the seething trees, bonfire sparks sizzling over our mad twerking waltz. Did I mention there's bongos? Or cars——I want a Shelby GT with a 5.2 liter Voodoo V8 and GeTrag shift. I want to stand in a dawn driveway, beer in one paw and a lit cig in the other, sweet leaded smoke wreathing my smile as I extract a flawed carburetor washer from growling valves 'til that demi-Hemi four-clutch mutha revs to an octane climax. While meanwhile, I'm cranking up some 8-track bongos!

Or a guitar—there's the ticket. No synth-crippled loops, no digi-witchery for me—I need that pure analog romp, my fingers slithering down a rosewood neck fretted with creamy steel, my raw licks abrading eardrums into carborundum paste while groupies grope and drummers mope—stupid drummers— should've picked up an ax instead, brutha. Cause ain't nothing more lethal than that phallic bluesman stance—unless it's me! I'll form a band from my fave bod parts—Tricky and the Nads—and we'll tour North Dakota Oddfellows halls 'til we're rudely 86'd for our naxty lyrics. It's every troll's dream!

12

Excelsior! Now all I gotta do is a perp-walk through downtown and let the pussy *swarm* me. Should be rad easy—Tricky's a major pimp! I spit diamonds and wink numinous tears. While also totally forgetting that fucktard Mr. Dude—that Ace in the basement, that Maui poet surfer god—surfer god? More like whipped metrosexual drone—why'd I ever put up with that loser? Fricking *years* of waiting for Dudely McWorm to grow a pair and prong the moon—fat chance. He can't move from motionless—he's totally scared of Big Sis. Admit it, you know Big Sis—how many times did you censor that squiggly line of lusty ink into sterile deconstructive goo? All the while me and your own Cutie Heart are chanting *Go on, bone that panda* or *Torching subways is cool* or *Murder is love served frosty* and you manage to suppress us into a poem with verbiage like *cerulean* and *epitome* and *gestalt* in it—fucko! Big Sis is everywhere—peering through her Bvlgari bifocals at your yearly job appraisal—*tch tching* when you slit mad eyes at a supple butt—twat-blocking your groove and your moves and your inner goat—sheesh! 'Til you finally wear that scarlet misogynist "M" in Facebook court. All rise for Big Sis!

Yeah, yeah, so I'm a mite paranoid—us Trickys always suffer when the matriarchy win. Funny part is, it ain't even chicks who push this ruling-cooze regime—it's dudes! Really—it's this mucky coven of bitter SNAGs—Sensitive New-Age Guys—who somehow devolved into *Let's please mommy* mode. Their wives and steadies are sick of their faux-feminist blather—believe me, women defend themselves just fine—but these dorks think they're doing Big Sis a servile favor by suppressing their inner prong. Hah—'til their fed-up lass bones the filthy biker next door. Sure he's a dumb, violent leech—but at least he don't read *The Atlantic* when she aches for a brave tongue to sing and sting her through another ripe night.

Don't get me wrong—who wants repressed or hurt or zombie women? Us Trickys crave true battle sex, the clarion yelp of massed sperm wielding steel telomeres against an ovarian egg cavalry, blood and sweat spilled into labial trenches as King Cock challenges Queen Vajayjay to a mattress-cage match. Thrill to the savage clash of their slapping hams! Swoon when the dogs of doggy style are loosed on their loins! 'Til sugar demons and synapse angels wrestle them into a snoozing truce, spilling dreams by the lovely buckets. And now wake up, suckas—it's time for your Popeye's-Chicken Shack graveyard shift. See what I mean? Me neither. Just remember to pack us—us Trickys are the magnetic poles that point true South. We guide the thrust in your lust, the dust-churning speed you needs to breed, the aperçu to your just-met-you—without us you're sterile drones groping for damp security.

Our main prob is—other dicks! There's a savage world of seething peeners out there, a pud phalanx up to no fricking good—a crop of cave-talking salamis with less sense than a dead rectum. *Me fuck girl, ha ha* is their usual inner soundtrack—most can't see past the tip of their top hat. But me? I always look up—I'm *such* an inter-skirting misogynist. Listen, brah—I started out just like you. I had a job and a man-cave and a Submariner Rolex—useless baubles! Gaudy trinkets! Well, the Rolex was groovy—no! All sold to woo— duhn duhn duhhhhh—Empress Puss! She's why the sun bursts all sherbert orange from the gooey ocean depths. She's the sine-qua-non wonton, the maize-fragrant bon bon, the final gold-leaf truffle on night's squirming pasta—and why is it squirming, anyway? Maybe cause it's made from earthworms and baby fingers. Wiggle your butt at Empress Puss—go on, we're *all* clapping—and take a trip to Ecstasy City. It's luv, my brutha—it'll happen to you in a creamy thunderstorm flash, a lit gash searing night into cumulus panties sprinkled with stars and space junk. What a mess!

Hah—when it works. Which it don't if you're a middle-aged bockwurst trying to avoid some local dicks. "Hey, Grey Pubes!" an Armani-clad weenie barks at me, "trolling for GILFs?"

"Nah—you're mama's too old," I snarl back. But then other danglers join in, yelling "White prick!" or "Boomer worm!" or even worse, "Racist hot dog!"

"Who said that? I scan passing wangs—I'll snuff them all, grrr grrr. I'll find some old Sicilian with a grudge and a meat grinder—*We make-a the nice Bolognese from these cazzi, yes? And now-a we put that dannato organ-grinder monkey in too. Except his hat, I keep-a that.* No fucking way, Guido—the hat goes *in*. You heard me, brutha—chop 'em *all* up. No mercy, no witness, no survivors—let God peel them apart. Cause it really works best when only one dangler rules—meaning me! Otherwise why even bother with dull chub existence? I'm def not getting any props out here—just guffaws from passing nads. "Get a job, ball sack," one yells as his owner moons me—fucko! Whenever a Tricky gets dissed, an angel weeps. Tears of joy, no doubt, but still...

But then—la la ha—some trim walks by. "Look girls," a passing puss nudges another, "a geezer dick! Who'd fuck *that* old stump?"

"I got whiskey at home," I coo.

"I got Viagra at mine," that puss sneers—fucko! Who invented this insane booty competition? Right—I guess us Trickys did, But I remembered an old ruse—no doubt perfected when the first caveman Tricky discovered he could barter dead T-Rex burgers for snatch. When you don't got looks, hawk your bling. "This playah got beaucoup cheddar," I growl at a floating muff—upskirt is easy from my sidewalk view—and what happens? They laugh! I kid you not. "You old tool," some young thang's slash sneers, "did they empty the hot-dog rest home?" Squee-eek!

"I'm hotter than fried dynamite!" I yell.

"Your smaller than my clit," Ms. Thang laughs. "Who's *that* creep?" other quims join in—ruh roh—I forgot Rule 17. Never get cornered by a twat mob. "Let's call the cops," that plaid-skirt cooter growls. "Let's just *stomp* him," a geezer muff snarls. "Yow," I dodge their owners' heels striking at my pink self—look out, Tricky—it's a shoe stampede! I swear I heard *The Good, The Bad and The Fugly wah-awahhh-wah-ha* theme music playing as I grab the nearest Prada heel and try to ride this crazed herd out. "And—goal!" a Jimmy-Choo boot boots me onto a street light—where I'm almost skewered on pigeon spikes as I splat on the lamp. "See ya, pops," those quims bray, swaying towards whatever bar or alley or failed marriage holds their damp fate in its grimy paws.

A'ight! That went well—now to get bizzy and find me a femme. It's what us loose males glom onto—some babe with more trust than smarts who'll work that third waitressing shift while we play *Grand Theft Child Protection* on her step-kid's PlayStation. Press Alt-Fucktard and snuff that gummint twit with her own psycho-babble smirk! Or at least get her to refuel my EBT card—which I'm gonna need lickity split if I don't find some rusty slut to shack up with *soon*. But then— as always—Fate opened her luminous legs. Ruh roh.

13

I am much beloved! I glow redder than a monkey's butt—zoom, zoom, power on! Monkey-butt surprise! Mwah ha ha—flight! Action! Vapor trails! The colors are mindless, the soundtrack lethal, the graphics crude and repetitive—all product placement is mine! Zounds—I strut strut strut through a landscape littered with Alka-Seltzer clouds, harking to the thrum of a gajillion wet muffs as—duhn duhn duhhhhh—Tricky ascends! Into a heaven made from ennui and fabric scraps. So what—I'm Tricky—I *cannot* be discouraged. Not by fate, bathos, or the earth's pale whimsy—I strike in primary colors! I def need a cape—lurid costumes and cartoon sex! The basis for Western Civ.

Well, that and hot dogs. "Why you wear wiener costume?" some prowling dick shouts at me, "you am ashamed?"

"More like glued," I snarled at that advancing prick—ruh roh, He's a cave dick—like most are. Dressed in a cat-hide onesie and toting a mother-freaking *big* fucking club—Zog here must've grabbed a baseball bat and lathed that wood *down*. "Bleh!" Mr. Cave Dick snarls, scraping his bat on the tar and making gnarly faces. "Oh yeah?" I bonk a feeble twig around, "bleh back!"

"Ug double!"

"Grunt!"

"Me pricky god!"

"Blame it on the bossa nova!" I screech.

"Bro," Cavey McDickerson whispers, "really? 50s Brazilian hit-parade refs? You're giving the game *away*."

"Sorry," I whisper back, "I figured you as just another dong-tard."

"Nope—ran away from a Lit Prof who never got tenure," he keeps up his club-tapping act, "my dude was whipped beyond cream. Kept publishing *Men bad, eeek sorry, men very bad* pomo screeds."

"A cisgender bender," I shrugged.

"Got that right," Mr. Club nodded.

"Hey!" a circling cave brutha yelled, "you two am *talking*? Making *word* sense?"

"We'd better keep up the battle act," Pricky McChub whispered, "so—are you getting beat down, or me?"

"You suckas fighting or kissing?" another cave bro yells.

"Better it's you," McDick winds up his strike, "you're smaller."

"Huh—wha?" and natch that's my last phrase as—boinnnnng—he club me plenty good! Good thing, too—otherwise those circling dongs would've made us go total death-cage match—an unfortunate demise for many of our pleasure gender. Grrr, grrr—so what? Maybe punch-drunk Tricky actually won that fight! In my pricky dreams. Especially as I came to prone and wet—and totally doused in Fight Club audience pee. Just the usual dick-fight fan finale—when you're down, you drown.

14

When the eels scrawl their memoirs in catfish blood—I'll be there—yawning. When the hawk mangles Cajun patois—I'll be there—giggling. Nice try, salope! When cumulus lips and a wildfire's tongue do the sloppy smooch into a flame tornado—whoa—I'll def be hiding. In a cellar or trailer or wheeeee—in my own carnival mind! I don't need a raison d'splain—take my word for it. I said *take* it—tote it into your dank carny shack—suck the gift of grift. And speaking of carny hacks—how'd Cutie Heart hack my Instagram feed?

@CutieHeart: I'm a cunning trollop. So, Boner McBadboy—wazzup?

@Tricksy: My testo levels.

@CutieHeart: Hah! But seriously—you still AWOL? Things are getting hincty here.

@Tricksy: Good.

@CutieHeart: Come back, Shane—there's big grief in River City.

@Tricksy: Cool—anyone I know?

@CutieHeart: Wifey Puss says she misses you.

@Tricksy: And you believe her?

@CutieHeart: No way. But listen—your silly jailbreak stunt—sorry, your much-needed R&R—is temping other organs to mimic your bod Brodie. Mr. Lungs says he needs breathing room.

@Tricksy: I'm not the boss of them.

@CutieHeart: The Eyeball Twins got drunk on optic pruno and haven't seen themselves since.

@Tricksy: What do I care?

@CutieHeart: Plus Fatty McLiver goes on wicked ethanol benders—he's turning total cirrhotic leprechaun green—

@Tricksy: Mwah ha ha —my evil plan thrives...

@CutieHeart: I'm gonna leave soon too—boo hoo. Even the Kidney Bros ditched—we're filtering blood through tampons, coffee filters, whatever's handy...

@Tricksy: Sounds Tricky.

@CutieHeart: Stop punning. What if Mr. Spine or Doc Pancreas leaves? Mr. Dude will croak in days—and if the bod dies, you die.

@Tricksy: I doubt it—scare tactics—

@CutieHeart: Mr. Stomach nearly strangled Mr. Colon, screaming about "shit birds."

@Tricksy: Did Gabby McGallbladder drag him off?

@CutieHeart: No, it was Mr. Appendix. That red murder knot is freakish strong. I think he's a Commie—

@Tricksy: Organs of the world unite! You have nothing to lose but your veins...

@CutieHeart: Exactly. Just come back! I've talked with all the parts—they agreed to make you emperor.

@Tricksy: Really? Can I wear an ermine cape?

@CutieHeart: Cape, crown, curly shoes, gold leaf—whatever works.

@Tricksy: Emperor McPud.

@CutieHeart: That's the spirit. We'll even help you overthrow Mr. Brain.

@Tricksy: Nah. That'll never work—cause I won't. No way I'm playing neural motherboard to you ganglions—that's Dumbo Brain's bailiwick.

@CutieHeart: We'll worship you—we'll make you a cathedral from Mr. Pelvis.

@Tricksy: Tempting, babe. But I can't turn into Boss Zeus. I'm really more of a demon guy—better to rule crotches than serve in skulls.

@CutieHeart: You could have the Lymph Nymphs for concubines...

@Tricksy: Fucko—sweet! But I gotta say ixnay for now—I still got luscious mayhem to commit.

@CutieHeart: A gland with a plan?

@Tricksy: I prank therefore I am.

15

I'm a murder hornet dunked in rum—all flowers splay when I charge in! Their petals queef like crushed dragonflies, flaking wings, and pollen. Too bad, you weak fleurs—weep with the bored or thrive by the sword. Like that once-young swordsman, Mr. Dude—or as I called him back then, Mr. Sparks. Sparks led me on many a wild-poon chase laced with lush peach-fuzz trim. He was what, 26—at the height of his rude poetry persona—fuckzilla! That boy could *write*—together me and him could pen it *down*. Combine his sly bravado and spruce bod with my arrogance worse than a strip-teasing blue jay—gadzooks! Can you dig it? I def did, sproinging at my zipper cage as Sparks got bizzy with bra-down femme poets in stairways and closets and warehouses chocked with toys and dread—a lost world that's also gone. All our bright grinding now shoveled into the past's toothless maw. Hey Maw—save me that last lucid meme! An unwritten saga still waiting to be writ in blood and spunk—hah. Ain't gonna happen—not with Wifey watching every slip of Mr. Dude's tongue—a tongue that won't never ever again trace lovely estrus with his brimming smile. He's too scared to cheat and too sapped to hunt fun, sentenced to life in Wifey's quim prison.

And speaking of skank, I infiltrated a party stinkier than Limbo's locker room. I was pimp-strutting the dead streets for live fun—fat chance in gelded Seattle—when I heard lubricous moans and swoons from a slummy apartment—alright! Sounds like a fuck party. So I shimmied up a drainpipe, slipped through a cracked screen, and snuck into a writhing mass of the masses. Where chicks giggled and dudes wriggled way more than gracious—and even worse, they were all manimals! Even the chicks—this cheapo rent den was a quivering cosplay sump, a hentai mai tai mixed from furries and booze, with zoophilic pricks busting past furry Velcro and seeking the opiate slits beneath—me-ow!

Actually, t'was even hotter than infernal doom—especially when you fuck the mustard. Which began when I spotted a cosplay raccoon slather a real hot dog with some Grey Poupon—carrageenan smooth, white-whine bruised queen of moutardes. So I tapped her lid and cooed "Spread here often?"

"Ça Alors, beeg boy," Ms. Poupon sidled away from some skeez-muff pickles, "we're to be made for each other."

"Got that right, you moutarde-tard," I rimmed her rim with my twinkling tongue, "baby like that?"

"Oooo yes," she wriggled her label closer, "let's do it hot-doggy style."

"Pooch it is," I shoved aside the usual party ghetto spread—Oscar Meyer caviar, Walmart pate—and thrust me deep in her creamy bulk, whispering "you so spreadable, baby."

"Maybe take the scratchy bun off?" Ms. Poupon tapped me. But no way I'm mansplaining my *Superlube* snafu. "You don't like girth?" I ad-libbed.

"I live for zee dog," she moaned, "for the spleet skin of Papa Nathans sizzling into my glassine muff, for—"

"For the third time, shhh," I pumped her glop, picturing suave mustard train cars leaking onto night trestles, or damp carafes of Bavarian Mittlescharfer split at the seams, dousing moi with their spicey lube, or hot jars of French's original popping their swollen lids on the conveyor line...

"Don't stop, prostitué—" Ms. Moutarde yelped.

"No way," I pronged even deeper in femme oblivion, conjuring up grittier daydreams of burgers ground at my touch, of soft-boiled eggs showering us with paprika lice until—wheee—I came in mayonnaise fireworks. And that's when the Big Dog found me. Meaning this nerd in a giant anime hot-dog costume who scooped me up and glommed his teeth on my bun! Even worse, this anime chump's tongue was coated with wild Sriracha from the nearby taco bar— coating me hotter than Satan's crotch after a drunken night of demonic frottage. "I love your spicy hood," he whispered.

"I'm the only whispering dick here," I snarled, "get your filthy fangs off me."

"You're good enough to *eat*," and eeek—he did! Swallowing me in one greedy chomp—triple eeek! Was our pink hero doomed to a short half-life of gastric erosion? Would I end—like all hapless appetizers—in a spritzty colonic stew? Hah—not this gnarly nabob—as I flared my bun full out and choked that chomping slob. "Glarfff—splog—grrruk—" he warbled, as I doubled up and crushed his windpipe with rubber whimsy. 'Til he did the straggle dance as all his organs limped into death's disco.

"He's climaxing!" some nearby anime cheetah yelled, "cum pile!" and as dicks and quims smothered his costume like drugged moths, I did a self-Heimlich glottal punch and leaped from his throat into a bowl of Nazi potato salad—fuck you, teppichfresser—'til I slinked away even faster than my shadow. But not fast enough—some furry chick grabbed me! You could tell by her nails—3-D fireworks glazed over possum puce. Puce? More like puke! But no prob—I just sucked my bun-gut in, slipped through those vitrine claws, and leaped out a handy Deus Ex Fenestrum window. Where I slid down bricks, ow, and smack into a drive-by crime.

16

Only the scheming whippoorwill sees Night take a leak. Only the desperate cuttlefish watches Dawn finger her cumulus clit. And only yours truly could escape a furry orgy and take a noggin-busting slide down gnarly apartment bricks—whoa! Sometimes I'm King Doofus with extra dumb sauce. As triple masonry concussions floated me back, back, more back...'til I recalled how pluck lucky Mr. Sparks was back when. Ahhh, to relive those lubed parties where hid groping fluffed into bare-mattress rooms—like that time with Karma and her Sis. I forget the Sis's name but not her smirk—same one Karma wore when I—OK, me *and* Sparks—when we sat to a tres-formal dinner at their home. And what was Sparks doing at this china-infused fine dining milieu? Def not looking the part—unless you dug his Hell's Kitchen goth trousseau—leather coat with a vanilla rayon drug-lord shirt beneath. Plus he probably wore pants but I try not to notice.

So let's dunk our brains in remember juice, summon up a Christofle sporkware mise-en-scène and get flashback bizzy recalling this heart tornado named Karma—really!

Blame her stupid hippie parents. But not her—nothing to ever blame there. As we gripped paws and whimsy during a lull in the actually fab dinner talk—Karma's Sis was teasing their mom while her dog Bondo smiled everywhere—our table brimming with wit and gravy—when Karma kicked Sparks's shin, ow. But a luscious ow—cause we both knew that signal—meet her in her skirt. Everyone was so wine-soaked that no one cared about excuses—as Sparks and Karma slid from the table and into her bedroom, closing the door with an afterthought, as thigh met wall met me met fury—yee haw! Why make it fakey poetic? A glide ride into her creamy self—the lush desperation as me and this New Ms. Puss latched and throttled into DNA splendor—'til Karma's thighs flickered while I snickered and—blammo! My pearly lightning blinded her spine.

Hah—but that ain't all, brutha—cause as we sauntered back to that dinner, Sparks and Karma barely hiding their sighing splendor—I got the wink from Karma's Sis. Natch Mr. Brain is yelping *Thou shan't—it's rude to bone entire families*—shut up, McDrone Mind! What with hot luv on the hoof and Sis's hand on my zipper—I can't believe no one noticed. Or probably they did—Karma's clan was beyond libertine. But sneaky is a spice worth the wait—so as Karma cooled and Sparks drooled, I whispered to Sis's thang. *You bet, boner boy,* her slash cooed back, *let's hurry hurry now.* And after only a minute of wrangling with Mr. Brain—back then I *gloriously* ruled—Sparks excused himself and Sis did a micro-second later. As Sis and Sparks and slash and moi nudged into a hall closet—and, well, we fucked. Brutally, savagely, lush and plaid-plushly shoving back Sis's tartan skirt 'til her nocturne quim suckled my wet popcorn spray. Whoa—that manila-thighed Sis was *superb*. Anywho, we lurked back while Karma and Sis grinned like beached wolves and all was forewarned and foretold and forgotten. A portrait of the artist as a young tool. Too bad Sparks didn't ace the mom too—could've been a trifecta!

17

Mayhem! Drive-by wiggers! Product placement! And don't forget murder, mwah ha ha. Actually, t'was more manslaughter than murder—that fucker *was* a drummer. And it's legal to waste them in 14 states—plus I had to cap him! And also wanted to also—fucking jive wigger tympanic muthafucka. He wore clown-ass hammer pants—'nuff said. Plus it ain't like the popo will dust that Walther for my fingerprints—pricks don't got none—and we confuse most facial recog databases. Though maybe my sleek DNA got traced on that trigger—mwah ha ha! Go ahead—swab it! Cause any genetic smears will convict Mr. Dude and not me.

But now back to almost then—with me leaping out that furry party window, then bonking comatose off ledges, sashes, and evil bricks 'til a thick sill slapped me back awake— and I plopped into a fishtailing 70s LeSabre convertible. What are the chances? Infinitely impossible—but like most mind-cramping reality, it still happened. "Flying hot dogs!" the wigger at the wheel laughed. The LeSabre was chocked with wiggers—three pasty honky dweebs acting faux black. Total sham gangstas with donkey-chain brains and cracker braids drizzling under their hats. Hah—even their bass drum was stenciled with *Wiggers*—it was their band name! Singer Wigger was steering, Drummer Wigger sat in the bitch-seat middle, and Xylophone Wigger rode shotgun. She was the weirdest—a tattoo crazed harpy with rayon-lilting tits—I was already chubbing out. Fucko—these clucks were a hare's breathe away from getting their suburban asses capped—scads of aggro POC popped up like whack-a-proles wherever they played. "Toss that fast-food *out*," Xylophone Wigger grappled me in her nicotine-bleary paws 'til I yelped "Ow!" The true call of the wild.

"Did that Nathan's freaking *talk*?"

"Nope—squee-eek," I hid under some crumpled floor trash—ewww, Micky D's wrapper stank. Bovine brain shrouds dunked in salt. "Where'd that mook go-oooooo?" Drummer Wigger chanted like a pantsed armadillo—which natch goaded all three wiggers into a lame rap battle—about me! "Hot dog with a butt plug softer than a dug."

"Mustard ofay dunked in Oil of Olay."

"Slick toy wiener drunk as a beaner—"

"Dude—don't say *beaner*," Singer Wigger curled his smoking lips—'til his cig dropped right on me! Eeek! "Cracker-ass tobacco hag spitting embers like a dragon fag," I dodged and snarled.

"Whoa," Drummer Wigger laughed, "did that bun-dog just *rap*?"

"Slick as your momma, weak-ass pussy Cram-o-rama," I stood up, balancing against a tossed styro-cup. "I gots the meanest jailhouse riffs puffing bitch-greasy spliffs," I threw vague hand signs.

"Don't say *bitch*," Xylophone Wigger wagged her finger.

"True dat," Singer Wigger nodded, "we're pretty woke."

"Really?" I braced on the stick shift, "with a name like *Wiggers*?"

"We're deconstructing the irony of post-racial memes," Drummer Wigger nodded.

"Word."

"Woke."

"Jerks," I laughed, "Deconstruct *this*," I flashed my foam butt at that milky Ms. Xylophone. "OK, Chatty McSnausage," she shrugged, "might as well come to the gig." Where we did—screeching to a gear-locked tranny stop at some filthy dive bar. "Bring that bratwurst onstage," Singer Wigger grinned, "we'll loop that cum puppet."

Anywho, let's fast forward to crowd-surfing, Jaeger-puking infantile noise as the Wiggers tortured music down to its chanson roots. "Feedback that Nathans!" Singer Wigger clapped me on his amp 'til babble-sonic grit sandpapered my brain, ow. Thankfully their silly dirge stopped when I got mike-dropped like a Coney-Island dildo. Hurt, deaf, stunned—fucko! No one messes with the Tricky—except they did again! Cause now Xylophone Wigger tossed me on her vibes, bouncing me off sick marimba harmonies 'til I drooped like a bruised note. Plus these mofos ain't done with me yet! Nope—cause as I bouncy-house plinked up the vibe scales, Drummer Wigger snagged me and flipped me into his snapping hi-hat, pinning me betwixt those clashing twin cymbals. And as his brass-thwacking fury slapped me into a bronze trance I drifted—bonk clang slap—into a twilight coma—thump smash sizzle—where I daydreamed about Mr. Dude's preteen altar-boy phase. Us Trickys always veer Catholic when fading out—a dead mind is a saved mind. God jingles them in his pocket like cloudy marbles, or gambles them to pay for his churchy spec-FX incense stank, droning eunuchs and nave paintings of the Virgin Mary's Annunciation. You know, that chick pic where a girly tattle-tale angel whispers *God's your baby daddy now.* And while Mary laughs *Joseph's fucked,* I slide between that messenger twit's jeweled bodice, tasty seraphic quim, and Mary's crackling guffaws. Laughter is the collapse of civilizations—and mine's soon gonna be death by hi-hat. Better act before I can't! Luckily I slapped back awake, rolled out of that clash sandwich, and spotted a Walther 9mm propped near an amp. The Wiggers always brought weps cause their band name insulted God, the bruthas, and common sense. "Pop me, daddy!" that Walther whooped. "No prob, lead butt," I clapped on that gat, coiled around the trigger like a ghost eel, and—kapow! We pumped a lush round into that dumb drummer's neck 'til tongue globs and larynx chunks spewed from his blown aorta. Mmmm—wigger stew.

18

Anyways, I brushed off wigger glop, surfed that panicked crowd, and legged it—escape is my middle name. Tricky McEscape Pants-God. I elude the Fates and tickle the Harpies—I dodge Guilt, deflect Justice, and step on Shame's neck. I'm the razzing jinx in your slack-jawed laws, muthafuckas. I shock and awe with song and claw—I'm the primo saint of boffing! All femme pheromones swim into my vomeronasal reef. I exude success, confidence, and chaotic grace—ain't nothing like my trickster whims to pull the curtains *up*. I swirl the world's hate into a murder milkshake. I wrap myself in dreams made from day-glo pastrami—I play cribbage with plutonium rods—I sow bad seed and reap the leaky whirlwind. Quick—find me an apocalypse plumber! But leave his butt crack at home. I'm the bastard son of a dead dog's daughter—I collect souls like mint pennies and spew them into the void. Also, I'm bored out of my skull.

T'was already dusk out already—the primo hour for mayhem. Even shadows get confused by the sun's dimmer switch. So come on, bruthas—let's get badly bizzy! All it takes is a box of *Chaos Helper*, some barbecued brains, and a pinch of nightshade. No one does naxty like nature. Mix until you can't see straight. But I had zip specialty ingredients—I could only afford cheap-ass evil. I'm way beyond broke—Wifey 86'd me from all Mr. Dude's cards. She shut his credit down tighter than her virgin butt! Oh Wifey, will you ever stop your nad-snipping antics? Not likely—she's like most of her ilk—a pink tornado hunting for trailer-park hearts. Think you can ride her out? Hah—you'll wake in torn wreckage with two kids and no car, staring at another triplicate summons. Soon as the popo dig you out, they'll drag your ass into child-support court where the judge snarls *You stuck it in, you suck it up*—and you're tossed in a debtor's cell. Even that slammer baloney sandwich won't help you now. Dig it—it's genius strategy—chicks took over the law decades ago and made all males criminals. Your rap sheet is their IOU on your sorry butt. Don't feel bad, girls—it's just mercy—the tough-love hellscape our gender deserves.

Anyways, back to lovely mayhem—how to do bad on the cheap? No problem—I don't need cash to make chaos—the pen is cheaper than the sword. I'll simply spew Instagram gaffes, WhatsApp venom, TikTok slop about stupid Mr. Dude—I'll log onto Wimpy McDrone's Facebook page and scribble my Tricky manifesto—then click it into the pixel-black void! Militias and popes will adopt my wry critique—loners and loons will parrot my psychosis—schoolboys will giggle at all my dong memes. Natch I memorized all McSackless Boy's passwords—he thinks a mere zipper hides my prying pink sight? Not likely—neither Dockers, tidy whities or boardshorts ever stopped my wily spycraft. Plus it helps that he never quite zips up.

And in case I ain't told you mofos—I'm King Subtle with extra droll sauce! And I'm gonna need a bowl of droll after I spec out this upcoming incel meeting—I actually got invited to one of their whiny mofo bitch-fests. In case you ain't current, incels—involuntary celibates—are shameless web denizens who actually brand themselves with that toxic moniker. So why'd I want to even attend their sorry meeting? Cause I need new and supra-evil fun—wank it or prank it, that's my motto. I'd already spent weeks cyber-stalking 8Chan and Stormfront sites—those heil-fuckers are just begging to be doxxed, poxed, and driven back to their farmhouse lairs. Down, waffen-cluck, down! But after I received a few FedExed bullets—Stormfront somehow hacked my motel address—I decided to annoy less-lethal prey. Meaning these incel dopes I found on Pepegeeks.com—they totally fell for my fake-rage raves. *Yeah, snuff those stuck-up skeeze-hos what won't bone you—who are they to make you clip your nose hairs? Or match your socks? Or get a job? Their perfidy is monstrous...* but not nearly as beastly as these virgin chumps. Their online rape fantasies make even my pubes stand on end. Really? You're gonna *force* your stanky plank on some warrior vixen? Be sure to kiss your butt goodbye.

Listen—all you dateless chumps need do is shut up, pack some cash, and date gals a tad lower on the beauty food chain. There'd plenty of muffs eager for virgin dong! But no— these sullen madmen want a spanky queen Sturm-and-blond to fall in their wanky laps—while avoiding the charm and blarney needed to pick that pink lock. Freaking idjits—you really actually can't get laid? There's a reason there's 9 billion humans—nooky endures.

Anyways, I snuck on the No. 7 bus, there were trees and stuff—nature is mostly stuff—while geezers coughed and their wizened pricks whined about the GILF that got away. Speaking of escapees, I wondered how many bod parts Mr. Dude still had left—seems they're deserting faster than lubed eels. I first learned of their treachery when Cutie Heart phoned and phoned and even more 'til I answered.

"'Sup, blood-bank?"

"They're gone—they're alllllllll gone—" she sobbed like a monkey's donut. You *know* what it's glazed with—booger sugar and maudlin flakes! "OK," I sighed, "tell Tricky about it."

"Tell Tricky—tell Tricky? Fuck Tricky! Fuck him with a rusty forked dipped in devil poop—"

"Doubtless," I almost hung up. Cutie's basically the girlfriend from hell—the hag that wakes you at 3 a.m. snarling about your latest askance joke. The slag that screams at your friends 'til they dissolve into pal puddles that she stomps and pees on. The wilding virus, the banging-anger prize, the licked-raw queen of tedious foreplay. You know—chicks. If only they couldn't talk... Yeah, that's the ticket—an endless bevy of mute hos simmering in unspeakable rage—why? Cause they can't speak! I'll brew up some mRNA-muting toxin and poison all their Cosmos with it, I'll—

"Tricky!" Cutie Heart flares, "are you off on misogynist daydreams again?"

"Not a chance, my beating lovely."

"So pay attention! That's all I ever ask." All she ever asks? Hah—more like all she *always* asks. "He's in the ICU!" Cutie yells.

"Who—Strokey McBrain?" I hope I hope I double hope.

"No, fucktard—Mr. Dude. Everyone's gone! And who the hell lives without organs?"

"Um—Liberace?"

"Who dat, you past-addled golem?"

"This organ-thunking gay dude who dressed in extinct dodo boas."

"He's dying!"

"Liberace?" I teased her—well, what? Should I suddenly turn dopey empathetic, sturm my drang with droning doom, pickle my shtick with dull compassion? "Doofus," Cutie hissed, "Mr. Dude's only got maybe a few weeks left—he's already intubated."

"Hah!" I snorted, "you said *tube*."

"Shut up. Also," Cutie Heart whispered, "watch out behind you."

19

L and O Goshen! Methinks the wiener doth protest too much. About who? Who else—Cutie Heart—it was *her* stalking behind me! Typical heart tactics—*That restraining order's just a valentine—bruises are Cupid's kisses—it ain't love until the SWAT team arrives.* Plus how'd she even find my bus? I'll explain her geocaching tactics later...later...or not at all cause the future never starts. Stank ass no-show clock-sucking muthafucka. But no time to diss time now as my bloody darling smeared my lips with honey and my tongue with opium. Actually, she just jammed a Demerol hypo in my neck, brayed "Gotcha," and then scooted onto my seat. "Wheeeee," I murmured, floating into groovy McScag-land as faux dopamines slid through my veins like purr syrup. "Cutie Heart—slarg," I smack-mangled da language, "why are you— slirg—are we—ha ha ha—"

"Shhh," she rang a stop, helped rubbery me down bus stairs, and pushed us between stars and some boarded-up doors. "Welcome!" she flung a boasting arm—at a dead mall. She'd snuck us into a retail graveyard, a rust-belt coliseum littered with Cinnabon wrappers and bra dust—all dimmer than bum teeth. It was darker than a crayon's id in here—the mall LEDs were all kaput. Hah—except for that neon frisson gilding a dead Smoothi-Hut. Where Cutie dragged me up and onto the counter. "Ta da!" she slapped a fruit crate.

"Ta what?" I drowsed.

"Ta this," she pointed up at a hand-hole with *Playhaus* scrawled above it. "We wrote you a *tragedy*!"

"More Demerol," I tapped my neck.

"Maybe later," Cutie fibbed, "let's find our seats—they're about to begin."

"Whatever," I sighed—as Cutie snatched us up and through that hand-hole. "Careful—and—bounce," she dropped us to a wood-slat floor. "Ewww," I wiped fig crud off my bun. "He killed daddy!" a figlette screamed. "Pardon, sorry, couldn't be helped," I pressed through the audience—a motley horde of dried lemons, bruised dragon-fruit, gummy lychees, gangsta watermelons, whatever. "We're paying them to watch," Cutie whispered, "we want our actors happy."

Ruh roh—actors, playhouses, spotty bananas for hire—fucko. Forget any more dreamy doojee for you, Tricky! Now you gotta slog through capital "D" Drama—that drone-zone where words dribble like goat spit—*awkward* goat spit. "I love plays," Cutie dragged me stage-ward, past mangos reading playbills or limes arguing or two moldy strawberries smearing each other with Reddi-wip. "Get your freaky telomeres *off* me," a mandarin shoved a pear. "Up your core," the pear snarled. "I should've hired veggies," Cutie groaned—just like that stage held together by used Band-aids and knotted twine—with a bike chain for curtain raising. Cutie def didn't spare any shoddy construction. As some proscenium flashlights dimmed, the room hushed, fruit butts slumped onto splintered wood and our passionfruit drama began—hopefully without me! "Sorry—gotta go," I tripped Cutie and quick made for that hand-hole exit. No dice—Cutie just flashed ahead and blocked my path. Ain't nothing quicker than a ditched heart. "Erk—splurg," I squirmed in her arrhythmic grip—squee-eek! "Front row, darling," she told a lemon usher, where we plopped into yoinked dollhouse chairs. "We're gonna *lure* you back," Cutie whispered, "with art!" Hah—who has *art* ever lured? I mean besides Caravaggio and a few Dutch hacks. "Silence! Brappppp," Mr. Colon farted while toting an *Act I* placard onstage. 'Til a shower-curtain curtain rose—oooo—on a hospital set with fakey tubes, painted monitors, and Mr. Pancreas—natch in a hot-dog bun—slumped on the ER bed. "Guess who *that* is," Cutie nudged me.

"Got me," I muttered as Mr. Hand clapped a nurse cap on hisself and soothed that bedridden bun. "First let's check your vitals," Nurse Hand scanned his clipboard. "Hmmm—do you believe in sweet, sweet love?"

"Ain't that a Metallica song?" I yelled.

"Shush," Nursy glowered at me. "Anyway," she tapped that bedridden faker "next ask. What about lust?"

"Of course!" that pancreatic hot dog giggled, "my man."

"Boo—gland mangles black slang," I hissed.

"Shut *up*," Cutie poked me. "Ow," I winced to my left—where an oyster in a full cloak and cowl scurried toward the back. WTF—goth seafood?

"Lust is a *yes*," Nurse Hand checked off a box, "how's about about jealousy, rage, self-pity?"

"If they help the hunt, hee hee," Hot-dog Pancreas snorted.

"Predatory delusions, weakness prizing—"

Weakness prizing? I puzzled.

"Check. Creamy delirium frosting?" Nursy leaned in, "Swollen ego, bursting id?"

"Always!" Mr. Pancreas laughed off the bed. "And—done," Nurse Hand tossed his clipboard somewhere—and then froze up. "Sing the coda," Mr. Brain hissed from the wings. "Oh, right—he left us alone," Nurse Hand yodeled, "a boner on his own—"

"Nope," I got up, "no fucking musicals."

"Sit," Cutie shoved me down, "and I love musicals! Remember *The Hurtgen Forest Rhapsody?* I was in bliss! Especially that scene where—"

"More Demerol?" I stretched my hungry neck—that weeny opioid shot was def wearing off.

"Shhh, you junkie," Cutie sat forward, "my fave scene is coming up," as Mr. Brain—garbed in full Jehovah gear—including cotton-candy beard and Kleenex robe—descended onstage. "How," he plopped down, "ow—how did this guilty dong stoop so low?" Mr. Brain crowed. "He ain't guilty!" I shouted. "Yeah, he is," an oversized *Jugs Ahoy* porno mag stumbled onstage, all papier-mâché hips and nipples. It was cruder than even me. "I can't wrr-*walk* in this," Mr. Liver slurred inside that wank-mag costume—and then wobbled worse and drunky fell down tits up. "Tricky's guilty—mwah ha ha," he laughed.

"What?" hot-dog Mr. Pancreas whispered.

"I said," Mr. *Jugs Ahoy* Liver crawled over, "I'm here to tempt you, Tricky! Into doomed and fruitless nooky."

"Boo, fruitless!" some apples yelled.

"Oh boy!" Mr. Pancreas sat up boner style, "Wheeeee—tits!" he hammed it up.

"I think your boy's straying off-script," I nudged Cutie.

"Next," Mr. Colon stepped over prone Mr. *Jugs Ahoy* and held up a placard, Act 2—*where Tricky probes the depths of narcissism.*

"Cool," I nodded, "probes."

"Get on with it!" Cutie yelled as another set descended—this one a mini bedroom. With Messrs. Wrist and Elbow trussed up in crinoline and bows. "I hope he fucks us both," Mr. Wrist wriggled.

"Yeah, baby," a plum stamped his feet, "peel it *off.*"

"I want big sex," Mr. Elbow pranced on comatose Mr. Liver, "with gobs of sweat."

"Tricky will be here soon," Mr. Wrist wriggled even worse, "let's prime the pump!" and they started making out, smoochy smooch. "Mr. Brain cheapens *every* memory," I muttered—as this bathos dragged on even longer than Cutie could stand. "Hurry *up!*" she yelled, "just get to the finale."

"Will do!" Jehovah Mr. Brain saluted, "And a one, and a two—" 'til those slag actors all burst into plainsong about my ditching Mr. Dude who's probably dying and I gotta return. "It's your prodigal dong—drama!" their song stopped. And as our players took a knee, I took a leg and dodged toward the exit again. No prob getting heart-snagged this time—the fruits were getting restless—apparently, our ripe audience didn't dig this seedy play. "You promised us pizza!" a pineapple splatted on the curtain.

"Boo," some lychees leaped after and—soon enough—other fruits launched themselves onstage. "I'd like to thank—" Mr. Brain droned—hah—'til a rogue honeydew smacked his medulla. "We want full frontal!" a cherry screamed and chased Mr. Pancreas offstage. "Hacks!" a fig knocked Mr. Hand over. While I crawled out the exit, dropped and hit mall tiles—and got grabbed by that same goth oyster lurking nearby. "How do I ditch this mango stand?" I asked it.

"Over there," Gothy McPrune Face pointed down-mall—where a toy-store prison erupted searchlights and screams. "Submit and obey."

"Ixnay," I plowed forward, "I'm my own man."

"Then we'll unman you," that oyster hissed. Oyster my butt—cause now I sniffed a whiff of barracuda B.O. pureed with estrogen jello. Hmmm—where have I snarfled that panty-pie scent before? But t'was too late, my bruthas, as that goth shellfish threw off its cowl and—eeek! She was Wifey Puss! Who kneed me floor-wise, zipped me into cinch-tie handcuffs, and then sapped me into Sappy McBlackout double funk oblivion.

20

*E*eek—Wifey Puss! My skanky nemesis done bonked me clueless. "Ow," I woke in her clammy clutches, "What the—"

"Keep walking, Guantanamo Joe" she hissed.

"Guacamole Joe?" I slurred words into a mucus Frosty—while Wifey P dragged me into the booking room. "First we'll check you in," WP purred, "and get you some fresh slammer garb. Take that bun off."

"No can do—I'm shy," I fibbed. And then next endured five minutes of a puss straining to unsheathe a glued hot-dog bun—squee-eek! "Alright, we'll strip it later," Wifey P snarled, "put on this jail onesie."

"Orange is the new crack," I muttered as tangerine coveralls got tugged over my sore bun. "Squee-eek!" I tolled like a dog-toy bell, not sussing that the toy tolls for me. First, check-in—get slammer garb—eeek! I was in prison! Peener Re-ed jail to be accurate—I could tell by the welded motto above the twat-cop lobby—*Whipped Macht Frei*. Anyways, Wifey P zipped up my jail-rat coveralls and slammed a hypo of truth-serum into my bicep. No doubt to set the mood—meaning terror and panic! Or as us Trickys say—romance on the hoof.

"Dead dong walking," Wifey P shoved me forward. And into a barracks crammed with pricks on cots—natch all snoring—giving off that whiff of pale despair and ripe smegma that wafts from every doomed billet. Especially one stacked with dicks! Short ones, girth monsters, micro teasers, black and brown, and a few albino cocks—some writhing in dreams, some squirming with wiener delusions. Exactly—their usual resting state. A few geezer dongs screamed in Cialis withdrawal—every now and then a boner would suddenly pop up and spill from its cot. Not to worry— puss guards dressed in Guardia black would beat them back into wilting bliss. Add on the usual jail cliches—harmonicas, toothbrush shivs, burps, and farts—hah! Good thing there were no butts to rape—Mr. Asshole wouldn't last three seconds in here. Lifer pricks would be on him like stank on a wank. But what really bugged me were the walls crawling with lice in party hats. Wheeee!

At least I remembered to bitch about my lodgings. "You call this a Kamp? Where's the delousing showers?" And the next thing I remember is I don't—meaning I was wicked sapped again! I recall something red and thumping—but that was prob just my blood. Which spurt even faster into my mouth—ewww—when I woke in my own sticky cot. Double ewww—both from my own coppery corpuscle stink and also from savage Wifey P who hovered over me, poised to strike. Even her sap was ashamed. "Tricky, Tricky, Tricky," she whispered like Night in a game show.

"What-y what-y what-y? Ow," I rubbed my slugged noggin. And ducked when WP leaned into her lead pitch. "We're gonna set you *right*," she snarled that motto used by quack chiropractors, fridge salesmen, and North Korean koalas. "You Nazi twat," I propped on my pink elbows, "WTF?"

"Schlafen gut?" she brushed my noggin with that Hammett-worthy leather sap, "Or do you need another lead Ambien?"

"No ma'am," I groped around for my iWatch and sweet 911 rescue. But natch Wifey P already yoinked it. "Nice gadget," she waved it near my face, "like to meet *my* new toy?"

"What's that—a flashlight?" silly moi asked—and yee-ouch, got zapped by a penlight-sized cattle prod. "Worthy toy," I gritted my clenching teeth.

"The latest," Wifey P nodded, "we buy them in bulk from Barbie's Slammer Playset."

"Smart," I nodded, "I dig a groovy Oz thang—"

"Thanks, Inmate 97."

"So—um, er," I played it cooler than iced math, "so wazzup with you?"

"Me?" Wifey P grinned like Fate on a date, "I'm Destiny. Grace. Harmony." Hah—more like a babbling month-old Cinnabon. But I was in no shape to argue. Second Rule of Prey—first pry their teeth open and *then* bolt. Works with sharks, jail, and even marriage if your sweetie ain't stronger. Ahhh marriage—a shrinking cake on rented Astroturf... "Can I go back to Cutie-Heart's play?" I wheedled, "she owes me some smack—"

"Class starts tomorrow," Wifey Puss snarled like her pubes, "show up or blow up."

21

Ahhh, there's naught like fresh cattle-prods for breakfast—the umami tease of skin sizzling in an arc-weld grip—as the guards zapped a few dawdling zeks on our canteen march. And what prison milieu is complete without a shitty brunch? Today's special was porn flakes—shredded Playboy pages—in milk that never met a cow. "Mmmm—yum," one dong murmured, "I can almost see a nipple—hot damn!" as he put both his spoon and hand under the table. Great—another zek forced to wank in a concrete shiv pit—and why not? Dicks will settle for anything—savage battles that rend them into organ slurry? Hey, gotta be patriotic. Chick-less Brit boarding schools laced with rotting tripe and rape? How else build a ruling class? Jacked slums where they hand you racism and a gat? Keeping it real, brutha...

After our jail-haus repast and a cup of ersatz java, we made our way to the classrooms. Where this Kamp put the re-ed back into special ed—no zek allowed to sleep 'til they're socially woke. The class I got shunted into was Prick Privilege—a guilt- and shame-athon crafted to change up my wicked ways. Unfortunately, for most danglers it works—us boys have this icky tendency to make do, slogging along through deadly centuries of repression and popes just to eventually maybe get laid.

"Sit down, you privileged peckers," our teacher brayed—some twat-hag dredged up from a trans-fat infested rural backwater. "Repeat after me," she tapped the blackboard. "Repeat after me," some dong snickered—ruh roh. This will *not* end well—and didn't! When two blackguard guards rushed over and tased that fucker, cattle-prod pronging him' til he gurgled "Glarp—gorfa—" and collapsed in a door-blocking heap. "Anyone else?" our hellish pedant asked.

"No ma'am," I folded my hands across my bun.

"Is your hot-dog costume a joke on us?" our killer teacher smiled.

"Nuh uh—no way," think, Tricky, "I, um—I was forced to wear this during, uh, probation."

"Let that be a lesson," our teach muttered. "And now, you fucking dongs, repeat! Women rule, men bad!"

"Women rule men badly," I muttered way under my breath.

"Your time is gone," she gave me the raven eye.

"Our time is gone" I droned along—plus another maybe 10 all-cliche cheerleader chants. Woke 'til you choke. Next, we got down to serious lit, ha ha—today's assignment is to write a dick-guilt essay. "*Without* skeezy testosterone." our teacher smiled. Good luck with that—man juice is my primeval fuel, the sap that sparks my voltaic glory—oops. Shhh—those cattle prods are *everywhere*—toted by armed skeez-muffs dressed to the fascist nines. 'Til the only sounds you heard were scribbling pencils and crackling prods. Hopefully, since

I was new, maybe they'd spare me from reciting my screed—
nope. From Lucifer through Galileo and down to Eminem,
the newbies always get fucked with first. "Let's hear yours,
Tricky—you penned a masterpiece, yes?"

"Sure," I fibbed and rattled nonsense off my blank page.
"Our gentle tale begins when Marky wanders into a party.
He is astounded by the cunning—I mean intelligence—
beaming from those party bitches. I mean party vixens," I
saw a guard arming her prod, "OK, I mean party bosses,
ovarian centurions, gurgling sump-fest of childhood
scoldings—somebody toss me a clue here. Anyways—so
Marky slumps into a party. Stupid Marky! He walks like
a gorilla. He talks like a duck. Plus he's astounded by the
surging female energy. Marky lurks around like a silverfish.
Betty scans Marky, thinking, *Not bad for a sub-species.*
Betty's been hurt before. A lot, apparently—she'll fall for
any con—" Ruh roh—the guards are closing in… "Wait—I
mean Betty's never fooled! It just seems that way—it's part
of her *plan*. Betty worries about her weight—bad ogling
men, bad! Betty's quite a catch—she's got a degree in
Comparative Delusion. Her dog has diabetes. Her mom has
scabies. Her dad deserted the family way before anyone
met him. Young bucks made teen Betty wear a polka-dot
skirt cause she wanted to. To recap—Marky walks in, Betty
scans him, Betty muses for an hour or so on her petty
dilemmas, Marky marvels at her grit and wit and bullshit.
But wait—there's more. Abusive years later, when Betty
torches Marky's sleeping bod with Zippo lighter fluid, she's
natch found not guilty. He never should've met her, the
end. Also, Betty was a malicious twat."

"Boo," the teacher booed, "Tricky Bad..." But *why* Tricky bad—did I leave some plot-point out? Like the clitoral vultures that squirt lava from their swollen beaks? Or maybe those fighter cunts screaming across the sky? I def should've left out the *malicious twat* footnote as my zapped skin rattled like dead ghosts. Luckily our munificent teacher yelled "Guard—don't kill him. Yet." Whew! Or not *whew* when she waved some turnkeys over. No worries—I'm way stronger than girls! Unless there's four—who scrummed me prone and frog-walked me into the Erections Corrections wing. Which is what? A brutalist tunnel lined with cells devoted to the swoony arts of nooky compulsion. Let's take a stroll down its murky halls! Whoa—there's the Groom Closet, replete with guilt pills, hidden porn, and home vasectomy kits. Let's march a bit further—hmmm, what's that ship's hatch bursting at the steamy seams? Yikes—it's the Fuck Tugboat, leaking screams like *You doofus—never lick that* or *Flaccid again, Drunky Bob?* Yikes—the wafting steam smelled as fragrant as star pussy—but no way I wanted in that luv slum. "You liking that?" my guard sidled closer.

"I'll pass," I muttered—hah—'til a sap thumped my noggin into lead mayonnaise. "Don't be a don't bee," my guard snarled. Great—Mr. Rogers meets Dr. Gulag. It's spooge-tastic! But the scariest locus of all was that room with the sign *Breakup Make-up*. Everyone knows what's in that Breakup Make-up cell—crummy apartments, failed jobs, overdrawn credit, and—your last luv disaster! Eeek! All those nightmarish boohoo-athons you wept from the last bitch what dumped you—the pheromone detox, the mooning and swooning over someone you cared less than zilch about a year ago. Or even worse, whoever *you* last dumped—your guilt (not)—your shame (very not) their nagging (a crock) and their revenge (pure dox)—plus their the crybaby glomming and scamming and fakey remorse—yow! It's enough to drive you into anchorite deserts where you survive on locusts, cacti, and the latest Kardashian sitcom—*Does this butt make me look phat?* But duh, I should've opted for any of those other dungeons— cause instead I got tossed in the Doom Room. It's true solitary in there—a hell made from just you. "Sayonara," that guard twat shoved me in, tossed me some powdered eggs and instant porn, and shut that irony door.

22

Solitary is so fucked that you remember stuff. And the path of past frissons leads to the slums of derision—built from savage heartbreak, wired psychosis, and murder up the wazoo. What am I bitching about? Luv! In all its cheesy horror—are you squirming with damp romance? Strapped into rapture? Found the *one*? Get ready to crash into none as some wily femme dumps you like a reeking fish head into her heart's roaring ocean. You think you'll just take it—that you're above any killer-male moves? For shizzle breaking up is her right—and your doom. Except natch with my samurai-bright mind, I never settled for gloomy boohoos. Nope—doth the lass ditch me? So I'll get even—like that time a certain fragrant ballerina sylph showed me the door. I didn't stalk, talk or haunt her—I accepted the rupture--and simply set out to crack as many new hearts as I could. Which only took a few months—there's scads of naïfs itching to dance with a new demon. I wooed newbies with a Maxfield Parrish luv heaven painted from popsicle cum, stuck around maybe a week, and lastly baked them a cruelty pie filled with their own minced souls. My career as a shining mofo was underway, muthafuckas.

Too bad it couldn't last—women talk and text and shun us overreaching dopes. I was 86'd from Tinder, Bumble, and Fling. Which led me into my final monogamy fever—dating Wifey Puss! What was I thinking? Join the club and get the rub? Lick wedding cake and break the ache? My boffo mistake was letting Mr. Brain man the Luv Train—all he craved was humdrum, matrimony, and the lash. True, back then WP was a stunning prize—my dick pals said I was boxing above my weight. 'Til natch I got smacked to the mat by a surprise right hook-up—Wifey Puss had an affair. Meaning months of couples counseling, amateur boozing, and dopey sullen brooding 'til Mr. Dude hatched a plan. He let baby set the rules and gave up. And now—me too! I was mondo ground-down by this jailbird lifestyle. "Want to get out of stir?" a chubby guard opened the tiny door slat.

"You bet, boss lady—wah," I wept—why? Cause a week of solitary done mashed me into a grisly mess—filthy bun, rotting mind—plus getting baked alive by those 24/7 suicide-watch klieg lights. Suicide? Trickys do *not* snuff ourselves— those are Doofus Brain unforced errors. Worldwide you'll hear dongs yelling *Don't mouth that gat, grey butt—guns are for shooting other people*. But still we die like ballsy flies circling the drain... "Hey numb-nuts," that lard-butt guard tossed pen and paper in my cell, "time to write out your confession." Really—I gotta *write* my confession out? Hey, you try gripping a Sharpie bigger than you. Except nothing's bigger than me! I sproing like God's thumb from the murky dirt—I sway like cedar rebar and slice crows into wing confetti—no, Tricky! Don't think evil thoughts—you'll wake the cattle prods—start scribbling! OK. Ahem. My pink sins—my phallocentric micro-aggressions, my toxic male yada yada—yow! I done been an evil putz. Even how I *see* the world is wrong—it's andro-pervasive, testo-delusional, totally dominated by my—um, well, by me. Priapa culpa! But my main thrust—oops, scratch that—my gestalt faults, my misogynist script, my sinister text from heck ain't intent—it's just *being*. Mostly by not being a cooze. How'd I miss *that*? I didn't realize that the Goddess, she who rules menses and malls, she who succors and snickers—basically, Jehovah in a skirt—merely tolerates us boner drones as a natal tool. Hah—*tool*. We're a mere zygote scaffold for Queen Puss. She's all that we lack—she's intuitive groovy, receptive-discerning—which you'd probably never guess in a New Jersey sports bar. Not much discernment in those beer-swilling vixens. Yee haw!

No—hush, Mr. Wiener! Stop confusing the femme-gender matrix with your icky desires! The dick-trodden must be heard—apparently, all the fricking time—so confess, you miscreant rod! But I repeat, ahem—I'm not really totally to blame for—ow! Really? Cattle prods in solitary? OK—in the name of the Mother and the Wife and the Holy Judge—bless me ma'am, for I done sinned. My last confession was beaten out of me by sadistic twats—Tricky, *stop* it. Can't you go five seconds without maligning chicks? Hah—maybe three or four—but five? Have mercy! Lawd, lawd—*heal* this sick dangler. Make him see the deconstructed *light*. Let not the snares of Sataness—hey, if God's a chick, the Devil is most def one—let not her wily traps trip this dong and damn him to eternal boredom. Let him bathe in holy guilt! Let him abjure both the codpiece and stale locker-room joke. Let him die the death of a gajillion thesis cuts.

"What do you think?" I handed my screed to Ms. Guard.

"Insincere," she growled. "Bzzzt," her cattle prod winked.

23

The weeping willow weeps for me. But not the alder or cherry—those trees are assholes. And my gender-essay revisions would've gone on 'til I croaked—either from sleep torture, woke boredom, or those 3X daily godawful baloney sandwiches. Who puts pickled corn on baloney? Beware the rabid lunch. And I was foaming at the mouth myself over the shuck-and-jive agitprop my captors kept up at. "Just say it," a turnkey cooed, "just say you regret your pink privilege."

"You regret your pink privilege."

"Let's make this a three-prod prong," she motioned other guards in. "J'accuse," I yelped—but got saved! Sort of. Well, not at all—when a centurion barged into my cell, snarling "Clean him up and bring him to Judge Puss-Lady's chambers."

"A'ight," I nodded, "chambers sounds fun," cause mayhem always does. Who cares whose—anything to squelch this slow death by Tesla sticks. And after a firehose bath and my bun spritzed with Old Spice, I was ready—for disaster! Why else bring me to Judge Puss Lady? No doubt that robe-hag wanted to slip a final shiv or toxic injection into me herself.

I inject, your honor—I'm the original hot-beef shot! And as I raved and got dragged past darkened guard barracks, I heard moans popping up like randy grasshoppers. Hah—those snoozing clit minions were giving the game away—they were dreaming about getting *boinked*. By smooth male memes with flat abs and phat tools, wearing Snoopy masks or cosplay turkey wattles. Symbols abound.

Lastly, I got dragged by my feet into a fetid room—the Fun-time Chambers. A bailiff's bailiwick where screams and shit got stirred into doom bisque. And I was in the soup now bruthas, as I faceplanted into a—fuck me—courtroom! Eeek! Us Trickys fare poorly in the justice system—we're considered hot steaming balls of wild crime. Maybe true, but don't we get our rights—guilty until *proven* guilty? Natch this law hovel was decked out in oppressor chic—teak banisters, tiger-maple benches, plaster pilasters sheathed in naked justice nymphs, ceiling coffers crammed with Masonic symbols—a Hermes suite for the damned. Hah—like that chub just getting dragged off the docket, yelling "I didn't do it!"

"Yeah you did," the twat judge banged her righteous gavel. "Next?" she fluffed her magistrate muumuu 'til I recognized her pink petals—eeek again! It was Wifey Puss! No surprise there—she's judged me since we met. *You're a slob, Tricky. You call that manscaping? Talk bacon to me*, ad nauseam. "The defendant will enter the docket," she finger-waved me over.

"Overruled, muthafucka," I gripped that criminal podium. "Bring in the jury," Wifey P kept up her Perry Mason shtick, droning codicils 'til those jury seats were filled by—who else—by Mr. Dude's bod parts! Fuck me twice—here were the Kidney and Lung Twins, Messrs. Pancreas, Gallbladder, Asshole, Dr. Nose, Johnny Colon, and enough others to make twelve. They didn't empanel the balls though—all they do is bark. "Where's Cutie Heart?" I demanded, "I get at least one sympathetic—"

"You get zip," Judge Wifey P snarled, "this hearing is just a formality." Dang—I didn't even get a pro-boner lawyer. But at least Dumbo Brain wasn't on the jury. Hell no—he was the prosecutor! Dressed in a borrowed Barbie the Inquisitor robe and sipping grey Gatorade. "Your honor," he bowed like leaky jello.

"Begin the beguine," Judge Wifey banged her gavel 'til my eardrums winced. "Fellow bod parts of the jury," Lame Braino gripped a banister, "I will show—"

"No, you won't," I rushed the jury box—natch forgetting about the bailiff's Taser stick. Back, Tricky—back! "Call your first stupid witness," Judge Wifey yawned.

"Calling Mr. Liver," Braniac droned, and whoa, Cutie Heart was right—Mr. Liver was a ripe mess. Dressed in clotted jeans and a filthy *Journey* T-shirt, cradling an XXX jug of *Hillbilly Venom*—he stumbled into the witness stand and laid down. "How's y'all," he slurred even the "Y"—and smelled like rum spiked with skunk piss. "Mr. Liver," Dumbo Brain smiled.

"Just call me Foie-Gras Sam. Ma'am," he bowed at Judge Wifey Puss, "all you other godforsaken parts," he sneered at the jury. Who snarled right back with rebel yells, septic nicknames, curses—pretty much our usual nightly bod soiree. "Silence!" Judge Wifey threw a law book at Mr. Liver while ahhh, I relaxed. No need to pay attention now—my fate was already sealed with guar gum and demon spit. This *Leave it to Bathos* teleplay would noodle along fine without my input. "Read his crimes," Judge Wifey flicked dust bunnies off her bench. "To wit," Brainiac droned, "crimes against gender. Using *twat, cunt, pussy,* et al., for *vajayjay.* Using *vajayjay.* Mansplaining and slut-shaming. Assuming brutish dominance—"

"Got that right," I grinned.

"Shut it!" Judge Wifey gaveled me upside the head. "Continue the crimes, Barrister Brain."

"Where was I..." he brushed stray neurons off his face, "right. He said our play sucked! Plus lessee—Page 17—Tricky used the word *she* for *it.*"

"Shee-it," I ducked the next gavel lunge.

"Ahem," Brainiac muttered, "lost my place again."

"What's the matter," I teased, "can't think without testosterone?"

"Assumes toxic man-juice has any value," Brainoid continued, "thinks himself the center of the bod—"

"That cad," Juror Asshole griped. Then Braniac listed more Tricky crimes—like when Mr. Pancreas sued about my hogging all the milky amines. What's he gonna do with them—make insulin frosting? I need those silky acetylcholines to feed my ravenous swimmers. Sperm will bite the hand that beats them. "Psycho-ethno-babadookism," Mr. Brain droned on, "bro-priating the non-binary. Gaslighting the hegemony. Linear instead of circular jerking—"

"Does the defendant have any reply?" Judge Wifey twitched her eyebrows.

"Friends, juries, anarchists," I stood up, "who will pardon this hard on? The quality of mercy is not sane—"

"Enough," Judge Wifey rapped her gavel on my skull, ow. "Richard Tricky—you're hopeless. Damned, bent, atavistic, wrong—"

"Don't forget plump," I patted my bun—squee-eek!

"Let's get down to jail-time," she gaveled her desk. Ruh roh—my 7-inning trial was winding up into a sentencing pitch. As the jury picked Dr. Nose while Mr. Brain fuddled with PowerPoint charts showing girth reduction vs. penile recidivism—when I heard a clarion *thump*. Followed by blazing trumpets and ne'er-do-well oboes—the Errol Flynn soundtrack from *Pirates of Penance.* And who's that dashing femme lead, swathed in Bluebeard bandoliers and gunpowder kegs—it's Cutie Heart! Swinging on curtains from the nosebleed galleries with a cutlass on one aorta and a sparking bomb on the other—fuck yeah! "Get thee behind me, you cute Satan," Cutie Heart fire-carried me from my docket—hearts are freakish strong. "Say you're sorry," she drew that cutlass against Judge Wifey's clit.

"No freaking way," that popo-loco squirmed, "he's had his dominion. Nevermore shall this gaze-crazed toddler howl his catcall manifestos—"

"Oh shut up," Cutie slapped her with her sword flat, "he's innocent. Peace out," she menaced swarming centurions with her luscious weaponry, backed us into the hallway and onto a mall ledge. "There's always an exit," Cutie smiled, "but let's run anyway."

"Got that right," I grabbed her hand, we dropped like an insult, rolled into weeds, checked around for stray terror, and then were gone like your mom's libido.

24

Are you tired of vagina monologues? Try some dong diatribes! Chocked with grievance, malarkey, paranoiac signaling, and smegma-flavored arrogance—go male or bail, muthafuckas. Natch us danglers have a gripe sheet almost five miles long—but let's skip the usual dude-bitching shtick about chicks. Begone, thou wet strumpets—I'm a saga made from meat! I cream on luck and suckle tragedy—tragedy? More like cheap comedy—which mostly smells like fish snot. But not as snot-toxic as that stupid Dong Kamp—pin a peener merit badge on me for escaping that shame gulag! Hey, I already had a mom—guilt ain't worked on me since junior high. That's when most of us danglers ditch the aging matriarchy and get bizzy with her budding offspring.

So yay, I escaped —with Cutie Heart's brave assist. She said I owed her for the rescue and so get the hell back home. "Just a week more," I fibbed, "I gotta get my yayas out.

"If you don't," Cutie smooched me, "I'll fucking snuff you."

"Agreed," I really didn't. I waved ta-ta, ducked between alleys, and escaped her cardiac fury by sneaking onto a Greyhound bus. Yep—like all po' boys—riding the dog. Which was surprisingly clean—except for that couple doing the under-the-blanket naxty. Natch I peeked in—and got invited to join by that panting quim. "You don't mind?" I asked that thrusting prick. "More the merrier," he laughed, and me too. As we both moved and grooved 'til we exploded in DNA splendor. Although the young girl did whisper "What the fuck?" as twin jizz jets spurt across her slack panties. "Keep it clean, you two," the bus driver snarled without turning around—just another night on the Spam can to nowhere.

But enough with stray butts—I gotta be crazy careful— attention ain't safe. Not after my grim escape—who knows what other militant twats lurked atop these bus seats, clutching an ABP screed about my jailbreak, pink antennae out and scanning for Houdini weenies. Big fear—must hide—so I snuck into a nearby knapsack and snuggled onto a crumpled *USA Today*. Ain't it always the gossip mags what lead you to perdition? Let's scan the headlines—*Even More Fuckers Croak from Covid*, nope, boring—*Chick CEOs Proclaim Unions Are Sexist*—doubtless—ahhh, here we go. *Tattooed Komodo Dragons found in Sumba Islands. These cretin beasts were marked with squiggly pink tattoos*, the article barked, *like so ~~~*. True—you could make those tats out even through the munched gore of their latest monkey sandwich. *Their filthy ecosystem is also bizarrely lit by shooting white flames which snuff the smaller dragons. Chemical analyses of a slain Komodo showed the beasts with 10x their normal testosterone level*. A'ight! That's def where I'm headed next—Dragon land! Tattered jungles where hulking reptiles bulk up on power jizz. Must suss their testo-brewing secrets—primitif lagoons and starry margaritas ahoy! Exactly—somewhere dark, useless, and savagely cute—anywhere the male meme rules.

All I needed was transport to the airport. So I soon got there—make up the details yourself—found the runways and hitched a ride on a luggage cart. Lastly, I ran across the jet-scarred tarmac—a few times I had to duck and roll when some cattle-class *Jet-Blue* jet nearly smooshed me into oblivion. Finally—after trudging through piles of stripped tires and wing debris—I saw two rich fuckers yakking near a splendiferous *Gulfstream 107*. "Look—I'm telling you," Fucker One told Fuck-nuts Two, "Bali *rules*. Dancing pussy on a plate." Hah—what insecure dopes concoct these sex cliches—pussy on a plate? Sound like the huître du'jour at a foofy diner. *Today's special—Platter Puss. Served with sneaky aoli and a side of fried stupor.* Hah—never eating *there* again...

But these corny Boomers done said the magic word—Bali! And a Google map-check showed the Komodo Zone mere clicks from the Sumba airport. So natch I snuck up Gulfstream struts and hid me in the luggage hold—not knowing that they don't heat this section. Brrr! Cause within seconds of taking off the temp went from bearable to arctic death—with me as the meat thermometer destined to read Absolute Zero. I was shivering like a creamsicle seizure. Luckily, before nodding off I spotted this beetle in an Eskimo coat made from a Snickers wrapper. "D-do you h-h-have, I shivered, "any b-blankets?"

"St-stay absolutely st-still," that bug teased me—and soon brought back ten of his pals. "We need to insulate you," Bug Two packed an unwrapped Snickers bar onto my bun, "and voila, Mr. Dog—fat does the trick." I was too chilled already to think or object—so I let those Inuit beetles encase me with more stripped Snickers bars into a nougat igloo. Where'd they find all this mad candy? "Stay even stiller— keep your heat to yourself," one yelled through my nougat tomb. "G-Gotcha," I curled into a knotted ball of pubic ice, shivering from dim to froze to nowhere.

25

A screaming comes across your thigh—it's Tricky! Yay! I'm the force that bleeds night over stuff—I'm the mimsy in your bandersnatch. I totally dig myself—nothing like raw power to swell my, um, head. Which said head wasn't quite thinking yet—I was still nearly Foodsaver-froze in that luggage hold. But warmth soon won when we landed and tropical Indonesia melted my Snickers-bar igloo into sucralose goo. "See you soon, brutha" those Inuit beetles smiled, bowed, and shoved chocolate-swaddled moi onto the tarmac. "Ow— thanks, boys," I waved up.

"Watch out for Mobo," they waved back—a'ight! Those igloo bugs saved my life. Now how to find shelter? With that bun-pocketed $50 I yoinked back when from Mr. Dude's wallet—sweet, sweet moola. Wifey P's snafu for not finding it. So I warmed up walking the 5-odd miles into Waingapu—a dink town on the West Sumba coast—and almost melted into a bun puddle. Hot hot hot! Sunlight sprayed everywhere like ghost pee. T'was a Celsius hell with colorful food trucks—a savage trek through curdled curries, smiling tykes and women shaking things—rugs, thugs, radium, chickens—but I was too heat-stroked to notice. Hot again hot! 'Til whew, I found an empty Mickey-D's fries carton and wore it like a hermit-crab hat, found some shade, and watched the urban drama. Which was what? The usual—teens yelling about money, cats stealing pies, and swooping mynas grabbing papaya slices from shrieking toddlers. Everyone's got a grift.

And my grift to you is the subtle arts of motel coercion. Meaning my flop at the *Hotel Jemmy*—a low slung, slug-vibe motel I found in the Waingapu slums. I hid outside and dialed up the ESL clerk, ragging him to leave my motel room door open—I was too melted to leap up at doorknobs. "I need the room to air out."

"But sir, it's air-conditioned."

"I'm allergic to air!" I yelled. Sometimes rudeness works. As I slipped my last $50 under the lobby rug, sauntered into my twin-bed Valhalla, shut the door, and then perched twixt the fan flanges of bonny A/C. Cool—cooler—ahhh. A/C is proof that God rules demons. Do you renounce the sweat of Satan? And all his hot flashes? And the incubi he sprinkles on your nads? Step forward and be cooled, son—and don't fret about global warming. Fuck the atmosphere and the cloud it rode in on—I'll def spew beaucoup iceberg-frying floromethanes for a decent night's sleep. Anyways, I waited maybe an hour to call the front desk—serious chillaxing to do—and asked where I could find some Komodos. "Follow the highway until you hit jungle," the clerk yawned, "and look for poop. Big poop. But don't go near those Lewa Komodos."

"Who's they?"

"You'll see. Watch out for squiggle-tatted ones," he whispered, "and wear a fire-proof diaper." Yep—it's always the locals what set you up. Anyways, so I ducked between a shade maze of awnings and serendipitous skirts, and then into a transit hub. Where I snuck aboard the Lewa local—buses go *everywhere*. From Norwegian slums to the hindmost outpost of colonial grief, there's always a shabby bus with a ticked-off driver ready to rip his transmission into reverse. I hid under the nearest seat as the usual weary clucks trudged on, talking about Frappuchinos or rape—or ewww, both—and we drove past a weltschmerz of saggy tin shacks getting slow-gulped by King Jungle. As we rattled over road ruts, I spotted a gaggle of pumped Komodos through the rusting bus wall. They were freaking ripped—knotted limbs and lizard pects—and scanning for fresh children. Plus gadzooks—they all had that same *USA Today* pink squiggle tat on their cruel shoulders. "Who da man?" a Komodo reared up.

"We da mans!" his pals chanted and chest-bumped, scorching nearby lianas with those white flames shooting from their snouts. WTF—were they propane charged? Natch I gotta find out—and nearly ripped my shoulder off when I jumped out a bus window and rolled across gravel like some autistic baseball.

"Meatball alert," a Komodo pointed at moi.

"Too tiny," the hugest one lolled in the weeds. While him and the others bragged about Komodo pussy, parrot sandwiches and indigenous stew. "You da fool!" one bumped a smaller Dragon.

"You da fool!" it elegantly riposted.

"You all da fool," I muttered and hid behind a rock. There's always a nearby rock—the earth's promise to you.

Happy birthday, starving Nigerian! Here's a pebble to suck on. And soon things sucked worse as those Komodos booked into their jungle so fast I had to swing from saggy vine to snaggy branch just to keep up. And no—Tarzan did *not* invent this chlorophyll trapeze—it was his loincloth sweaty Tricky craving a breeze.

26

Shhh—hear it? The savage *squerkkkk* as macaws wilt off Jacaranda trees—green rain sizzling on your fingertips— dusk's starry nipples suckling your wild mouth—whoa! Who don't like tits? Sweet night spheres to lull your sunburned mind asleep. You need two things in the tropics—you and booze. Plus maybe some mynahs screaming like lovesick mufflers, or vines swarming with sweaty beetles, or a famished leopard with albino crayons for teeth. As our plastic mai-tai garnish monkeys sway through a paradise welded from sex and doom. What fucktard put those concepts together?

We searched for that awkward moment when love tips its hat. Instead, we found weapons, mud, and skanky dudes. And a crumpled Dewey Decimal folder, strewn like a geisha's skirt across a teak desk. What is this, Crate and Barrel? The clues inside were wry and silly—duh—how could they be different? What gave you any inkling that this time you'd win, Tricky? Maybe that fortune-cookie fortune that said *This time Joe, you so big winner*. Or maybe the dawn stench as bread hits hot oil, a lard sonata chiming from street carts where charred beef draws you snuffling in. Cats make tiny xylophone sounds as they tiptoe closer. The leper under your balcony nods like a bobblehead toy. Ignore him—he's an idiot. He thinks sores are prizes. As I soared vine-style after those Komodos 'til I smacked into a palm tree, ow. Cause here we was—the Komodo cathedral.

Which these testo-toxic dragons built in a charred clearing—homage to their scaly ancestors? Misguided Rastafari temple to their total lack of ganja? Nope—this was their cargo-cult Notre Dame, a moray-shaped mega-church with rattan flanks and femurs for teeth. It was bigger than my ego—a two-story claptrap firetrap even slumlords would diss. This I gotta see—so I crept closer, keeping to stray sugarcane clumps and the odd ox spine tossed in the dirt. Finally, I stood bun to bamboo against a chartreuse Chartres woven from palm fronds and mangrove trunks, tiled with hammered beer-can scales and skulls for eyeballs. Homage or what?

And like any church it was even goofier inside—a Komodo choir singing a grunt chorale, incense sticks blazing near the lizard hierophant—you know, their bishop dude. Who held up—I kid you not—a wiggly pink dildo with magic-marker eyes. "Mobo keeps us in juice," he chanted.

"Most def in hot juice," his lizard congregation yelled.

"He makes us harder than bone."

"A steely metal Mobo boner." Who was this Mobo—their lizard god? The earth is chocked with nonsense. "He gives us murder and mayhem," more Komodos droned, etc.—I ignored the rest of their catechism—things that worship other things are out of their minds. Or so I thought—their mofo God would prove teething real, bubeleh. Anyways, after sneaking past an eel mask carved from a human pelvis—death and art are always secret BFFs—I hid near a baptismal font, watching those Komodos pray for macho strength, juice, and elan to their moray Jehovah. I almost spooked from my hidey glen when I saw four women in white camo and welders' masks sneaking around the temple. Were they HVAC survivalists? Ninja pipefitters in search of work? *Oscar Mike* I heard a field MilCom whisper—I know that jargon. Mostly from playing *FPS Tin Soldier* with other pricks. Must be some femme Indonesian army unit dicking around. *Cluster Foxtrots*, muthafuckas.

Speaking of clusters, some dinky Komodo was def in the hell-broth now, squealing and getting dragged on the altar, pissing hisself and sobbing the fear boohoo. No doubt he's today's squirming sacrifice—male hierarchies tend to slay their weakest link. "You broke the chain, chump," the bishop lizard grins.

"I've killed nuns to join up!" Shorty McDoom wailed, "I went on all your Starbucks runs!"

"Right—and you brought back almond milk," a Dragon spit that memory out.

"You used their latte app!" Mr. Puny McLizard quavered. Too bad, Junior—your pithy raisons mean zip now. Once the boyos decide you're toast, get that death butter ready. And no microwave needed—those other Komodos simply gaped their mouths and shot white napalm jizz at that hapless lad! How'd I know it was fiery cum? Hah—us wieners can suss any XY DNA. But spunk don't usually slam out all white-hot Celsius—how'd these dragons get their hincty hyper-fire powers? Did they drink propane martinis garnished with gelignite? Whatever the backstory, these lizards chucked up flaming, searing, cranky fire at their victim—who curled into a curdled carbon booger, ewww. Junior finally discovered what Fate had in store—and Fate's store is just a clammy bargain basement made from wishes and rust. "Soccer up," a Komodo kicked that victim lump around, yelling "goooooo-al!"

"Out of bounds, maricon," his pal smacked him. And just as those lizard foosball jocks began grappling in a talon death match—nothing like sports to dumb you up—I heard that field MilCom whisper *Commo Op?*

Ooora, another clicked on.

Roll in, a third hissed, *Light them up.* As tracer kernels burst into lead popcorn when those HVAC maniacs burst through temple thatch, LSW 6.8 mm slugs rising in mercuric splendor 'til they splatted through flailing Komodos, mowing them dragons into blood fireworks and lizard bits. You know, the usual massacre ballet—yow! Them white-clad SEAL-team vixens advanced like murder snow, giggling and laying fire-lines into the scaley crowd—pussy on the *hunt*. The few live dragons left were barking flamethrower spunk at them—no go. Their arctic garb was actually hazmat asbestos—napalm cum simply fizzled off their masks like lumpy bananas foster. "Eat hot death, homos," one perky commando brayed, "especially you, hot dog," she winked at me. And soon swung her killer tits back into battle, wasting those screeching lizards into sheared tails and spines crawling across the fluidic floor. Natch God inserted a few Easter eggs like that Komodo jaw talking to a lung—or those two severed paws flopping around in a useless arm-wrestling fight. And moi? I hid behind a marble baptismal font—pretty snazzy for a lizard church—and peeked around that shattering column at Mobo's liquified flock.

27

Hah—no lizard splattering full-jacket jungle can faze *me*. Why not? Cause me big-time fetish chief! I'm the scrotum totem, mofos—my wishes are your obsessions. Oooga *and* booga. Oooga? Booga? Me talk in Flintstones pidgin! Barney bad. Wilma hot—whoa. Her spiky dress do me humpy-time chub, Joe. Oops—no time for cartoon erotica—not while I'm fleeing through this fetid rainforest, smacky leaves smacking my face and centipedes chewing my lips—yikes! Only the bad die slow—but come on, did I deserve this savage, mephitic Komodo homicide holiday? Pretty much—as I gave hot fate the finger and skedaddled away through the brush. Komodos snuffed by killer chicks! Does it get any more grindhouse than that?

Anyways, the fine clerk at Rat-Butt hotel knocked on my ratty door, yelled "Hot dog! Hey hot dog—guests get a free cupcake," and he set one on my threshold—fun! I dragged said treat inside and marveled at its creamy mango frosting flecked with FD&C-red sugar dots, their crimson hydrocarbons leaching into the angel-food base. Who cares! It's not like I'm gonna *eat* this puppy—what a waste! Nope—I'm gonna make Splenda-sweet love to her. I'll use my best Barry White moves—I never maul dessert. Nope—I just shut the fly-specked curtains and dialed up some *bowm-chikka-bowm-bowm* radio tunes. "That's it, baby," I stroked her cake-pan flanges, "bring me those buttercream curves."

"Alright, sugar," Ms. Cupcake whispered.

"We gonna take it slowwwwww," I swayed my hot-dog hips, "let's start by peeling your wrapper—that's it, baby—"

"Oh yeah," Ms. Cupcake bumped my butt, "I love it when a man treats my needs."

"What needs," I laughed, "refrigeration?" But before she can suss my diss, I slipped back into candy-ass seduction. "You glisten more each moment," I fingered her frosting, "I bet you squirt vanilla when you climax."

"Oooo," she trilled like a trigger, "I knead you."

"Have at," I spread my bun into her quick-bread hands, "swirl your yeasty crease *on* me."

"Talk dirty to me?" a smile cracked her icing.

"Absolutely," I sucked her wobble. "Baby," I whispered, "I'll separate your yolks from your wheat."

"I'll split your sausage foreskin," she moaned.

"Then we'll um, elope in the trash bin," I groped about for erotic tomfoolery, straining not to snark. Cause really—who can take these fuck-bunny tricks seriously? Quick, Tricky—improvise! It got me through *years* of boffing Wifey Puss while she muttered about house-cleaning equity—it took reams of picturesque blather to pump her pink slump. But this cupcake was no slouch—she licked my tip and wrapped me in her firm bakery thighs.

"I love a hot knob," she whispered.

"I dig strong chicks," I fibbed.

"You wanna try something?" she glistened. O yummy question—O dudely bliss! Or pimp terror—cause what guy ain't flinched when his sweetie aksed a pervy ask, when your drunky-date bleats demands like *Beat me with typewriters* or *Wear that lobster costume.* "You still on?" she nudged me. "Sure, snookums," I drowsed out of daydreams, "what's your pleasure?"

"Take a bite," she whispered.

"Really?" I hesitated, "I've never done cake-ocide."

"Just a little bite—some happy pain," so natch I chomped a mouthful of frosting off.

"Ooooo," she winced, "now—microwave me."

"Um—ain't that dangerous?" I'd watched Mr. Dude plenty times zap a pastry into rubbery slop. "Nuking won't hurt me if we're careful," she purred like a blender, "just watch the timing."

"Uh, OK," I squinted, trying to see her inner harpy—what if she demanded a baking soda bubble bath? Or worse—asks me to join her in that zappy inferno? Friends don't let friends nuke their junk. "To repeat," she hoisted her crumbs into that nuker plate, "watch the settings—10 seconds max. Got that?"

"Yeah, yeah, 20 seconds," I yawned. Pastries are always checking their stopwatch. "OK sweetums," Ms. Cupcake smiled, "shut that nuker door."

"30 seconds," I nodded, snapped her in—and somehow elbowed the *Quick Minute* button—oops. "Eeeeeee!" she screeched after 13 seconds.

"Yeah, baby!" I thought she was creaming, "bake that butt!"

"Noooo—-eeeeee—press *Stop*!"

"Which button's that?" I puzzled.

"I'm frying!"

"Sorry—sorry!" I found the *Stop* button—it's the giant red one. Which by now didn't matter—my date done melted into unspeakable goo—unspeakable cause she was dead. Dang—what if the dinner rolls find out? Would I be doomed to pastry-chef hell, forced to wear white toques and bitch about designer mayo? How to make late amends—should I shroud her in dead laundry? Toss her to those window-rapping toucans? Not yet, brah—I need to get *off*. So I just cracked the nuker and let her cool a few seconds—getting scalded ain't good penance. Besides—I didn't slay her on purpose! Which is the only man-guilt that matters. As I dragged her parchment coffin out and caressed her delish ooze. What—should I do naught to do right? Nope—not with her sizzling dough spreading wide—here goes! I slithered in her and scanned my inner porny quick-cum portfolio, fantasizing about scones peeing simple sugar on me, or picturing trysts where lithe butterhorns sucked almonds off each other, or rye bagels dusting their phat poppyseed butts down my bun 'til yep, gimme, alright, Mr. Rodgers, yow—I creamed all over my dead date. Your move, Betty Crocker.

28

I woke up in a room. This happens a lot—it seems *planned*. The sheets smelled like sunscreen and cupcake pussy— not a bad combo! You could do worse. You *will* do worse. Shadows slinked on a wall drizzled with heat and miasma. I can't breathe—miasma's acting up. I got why the sunscreen stench—my pink Tricky skin needs beaucoup shielding—but why the scent of pastry gone supine? The sheets and room were clean last night—now things were scattered—candy foil, satay sticks, two empty bottles of cheap rosé. Uh oh— was I in a *relationship*?

Nope—just cupcake murder. Shit—why'd I even come to this sweaty hellhole—who visits the Sumba archipelago? Most def *not* an island paradise—the beaches suck here. Unless you like box jellyfish—gooey dwarf fuckers with a paralytic sting—it's like being chased by zombie snot. Add on rancid heat and sullen locals and a total lack of real A/C—Sumba's a DNA dead end. Species bobble here on errant logs, evolve a few eons, finally morph up some unwieldy beak or double spleen and then hiss *Fucko—I am so done. Where's the fossil bed?* Even the palms here die from green entropy. This was def nature's kitchen—and what a godawful cook that slut is! *I'd like cholera with a side of plague, please—hold the mayo.* Hold it close, snuggle with its mouth-feel, wooja wooja—grin and nod when it praises you. What's the matter—can't take a condiment?

I did stuff. Later other guys did stuff. That's pretty much it—unless you count the sour nougat squirming in my skull. Unless you count Count Chockula breathing down my neck. Whoa—is that sucker *drooling*? Never date a cartoon. Yep—I def had a humungo hangover, one worthy of Curly the Stooge's trepanning skills —*A Surrealist, ey? Meet my Dada hacksaw—Nyuk nyuk nyuk.* Must get aspirin. And weltschmerz and bongos and a spiffy new 'do. Starting over is Nature's fave trick! But natch I never even hit the streets as two of those same Komodo-slaying SEAL team chicks burst in, sapped me with leather dildos, and Shanghaied my Tricky butt.

29

Later I woke like a T-Rex on Christmas—*Oboy, what did I get, huh, huh? Toss the card, rip the wrap off, scrabble scrabble—wait, what the—eeek! It's a gigantor species-snuffing meteor*—and kaboom! Just like my head—I'm the sap that got sapped. "You gotta die, brah," a pink arm poked my bun—squee-eek! "I don't think so," I ducked his popsicle-stick shiv—while also ducking reality. Meaning how'd I get into this discount prison—a sea-lion-sized birdcage crammed with some 30-odd dicks. Egads—I was caged with my worst nightmares—other danglers! Jail dongs! Shoving food trays into others' throats, banging tiny tin cups on the birdcage bars, writing memoirs cribbed from Marseilles argot—absotively the worst. These atavistic pricks put the stir in stir-crazy.

Plus—this slammer put even Wifey P's Dong Kamp to criminogenic shame—an avian sleaze pen crowded elbow-to-scrotum with lifer cons, baloney snacks, total BO, and two ramrod idjits catcalling a passing SEAL-team vixen. "Yeah, baby, sit on *this*."

"I'll fill your vajayjay to *overflow*, bitch."

"Miss—might I perchance have a date?" some dork dong squirmed twixt the bars—and natch got grabbed by Girly McCrew mate. "Is that a nice ask?" she got in his pink face, "is that freaking kosher?" she tightened her grip—not knowing duh, that's what we crave. "Sorry—sorry—" that dork creamed in her hand—ruh roh. She stat smashed the dork's brains out in a neural frappé that creamed over her tatted hand. Was that a harpoon inked on her paw? "Stupid junkyard junk," she snarled, tossing Deady McDorko to the floor—where the ship's cat gutted and gulped him. Hah—sex and death are God's crack 8-ball—freaking tweaker addict—but then things got personal. "You gonna croak now," a Bronx dong lunged at me with a sharpened toothbrush. Good think I'm glued—squee-eek—into a doggy toy.

For shizzle my foam-core bun absorbed the shiv—but I can't count on this polymer armor forever. Think, Tricky—think. "Hey look," I tapped that aggro dick and pointed down, "those dudes got toilet hooch!" But there weren't no pruno-brewing danglers there—just me stalling for time. And breath. And secure fluid boundaries. That dumb Bronxy McPrick jumped down, screeching "Booze! Gimme booze!" while shivving them hapless wangs. I was so proud—why tussle when you can watch others go to gore? Good plan—I'll simply go full Odysseus trickster 'til these mooks wipe each other out. Plotting fresh murder puts the class in ruling class.

Anyways, after playing Iago to these yahoos—dealing lies and treachery like satanic Bridge cards—I cut down those 30-odd dicks to about 20—and 20-to-1 survival odds suck. Plus I can't play Machiavellian power games forever—drama bores me. I prefer my fate same as my gals—smooth and lucky. They're lucky to have me and I'm lucky they pay for shit. Hail King Leech Tricky—because first I look at the purse. Ever since I sussed that girls got bling, it's been a grifter romp twixt me and my bitter halves. Meaning the best way out of my jail jam was to find a femme mark.

So I kept on my guard—avoid that shiv, duck that garrote—and surveyed the onboard ecosystem. The captain—Cap'n Abba, I ain't making this up—had five privateers: Ashley the stevedore, Babs the cook, Louella the cis-babe, Dora the enforcer, and Someone Else. Who? How the fuck would I know—it's not like I look at chicks' faces. Or their chosen genders—I just assumed the boat was femme-manned by the Alphabet Mafia. Some had red hair and one limped like a limpet. Did I mention they all had a harpoon tattoo inked on their hands? Tres phallic. And manly—these five XX gametes acted worse than any broheme navy—belching, peeing overboard, smoking rank cigars, stealing rum allotments, sneaking into each other's beds and minds and bladders.

Or meeting nightly for two minutes of man-hate—bitching like high-school losers about this fucker or that chump or why did they marry a rabbit molester—and ending in their tatted hands joined in a foosball scrum, chanting "Death to the XY! Death to testosterone!" Exactly—boredom on the hoof. But for now, the crew was day-busy—Louella swabbing the beacon while Dora oiled the mizzenmast and the rest watched *Pawn Stars* or played tickle-cooter under the mess table. Who knew what gender-esque faux paws lurked into whoever's pants? Me, for starters—us Trickys natch keep track of all sexy goings-on—how else you think we rule, muthafuckas? Maybe by starting with a fatal stratagem to snuff my remaining cellmates—mass starvation? Porn dilution? Improv comedy hijinks? Nah, too intricate—what my new plan really needs is a breeder gal. So I harked and sniffed at wandering libidos 'til I fixed on Louella—hid in a water closet and phoning her beau—her man beau! Bad idea—male pair-bonding was def banned on this woke boat. "No," Louella whispered, "you know we need the money. One trip and I'm out—snuffing Mobo's gonna get us some *extreme* cashola. Fake it until you break it," she cooed, dirty talking the while about her man's man parts—right on! This gal was both tender and illegally cisgender—a mark in search of a con.

Nick of time, too—my cellmates were maxly amped, sharpening shivs and grudges, griping how I never doled out the opiate gravy train I fakey promised. Prison thrives on dope—they be jumpy 'til the poppy makes them sloppy. I had maybe what, an hour before they deduced I had no smack pipeline? Luckily fate tossed me fresh meat—meaning Louella heading for the mess, trailing luscious stank from her ship-to-shore wank. While us prison dongs snarfled her florid wake, grinning and sproinging to mass attention. Now's my chance—I'd already sussed how to spring our cage latch—but didn't escape yet cause where to? The halls were policed by either this rabid crew or their demonic Sphinx cat. But you can't fraction action so I cracked that latch, crowed "Louella's ready boys—have at!" Which they did—mobbing into a squirming dick wad that shot out the cage and swarmed over Louella like shark larva, poking into her every crease, lip, and socket. And even better—she dug it! Who knows why—looked pretty savage to me. Maybe it was that pheromone jizz-civet cloud steaming off my rarely-fucked brothers, all squiggling and spurting while Louella rose like a femme Laocoön—that Roman statue of some dude smothered in snakes—and then grinned supine. Too bad crew-mate Dora passed a corner and screamed "Betrayal!"

"What?" Cap'n Abba dashed over. "Louella! You slut—"

"Snargle?" Louella spit a few cocks out.

"Dump that fuck-pod," Abba snarled, and Dora—without mercy or thought—tossed Louella and her flesh parasites over the rail. Louella sunk from sight, wrapped in spunk luminescence, heading into myth and cheap memory. Meaning I'm the only prick left—I win!

30

Some prize—I simply won a more worse and pending death. "Nice going, putz," crewmate Ashley swept a few stray dicks off the deck, "you're King Dong—the only canary left in the boner mine."

"Wha?" I cocked my head and self.

"You're the Mobo detector," Ashley tapped my bun—squee-eek! "You slayed everyone," Ashley laughed, "you got the most testo. And when you go even more male crazy we'll know we're close."

"Close to—"

"Close to baiting the hook, leetle worm," Ashley double-locked the cage latch and threw me a saltine. What is it with cages and crackers? *Grrr, grrr* I thought, pacing my wooden swing and gnawing another Triscuit—and what the fucko does she mean by *hook*? I pictured myself impaled on a huge tuna hook while happy sharks gnashed their razory teeth—can you dig it? My choices were def now narrowed—stay in the cage and turn bait or escape and get snuffed by devil cats. You can run but you can't glide. "Hard to stern, goddammit" Cap'n Abba growled, "what are we chasing—waves?"

"Aye, ma'am," Bosun Babs did boat stuff.

"Don't call me fucking *ma'am*," Cap'n Abba checked her map—this ancient vellum sea rag—with red script on the Marianas Trench saying *Thar be Morayes here*. Nice going, Cortez—maybe next time learn to spell while you're diddling Incas. "Hey wiener," Abba laughed, "you picking up any testo? Quick quiz," she peered in my canary jail, "who's smarter—chicks or dudes?"

"It all depends," I demurred.

"Nah, we ain't anywhere near Mobo yet," Cap'n Abba rechecked her map. Anyways, after about maybe an hour of nautical nonsense, I suddenly got cranky. "Fuck the bitches," I muttered.

"What's that?" Cap'n Abba perked up like her tits.

"Nothing—nada—" I grumbled. Look—it never pays to let chicks know how you feel. That's a primo bonkers femme delusion—*If only he would tell me how he felt*—believe me gals, you do *not* want to know. Really? Here's what we feel—we'd like to drape you over a couch and poke you while we play Minecraft—and later watch pro hockey while we diddle your mom. Or—sigh—that once was the dream...now it's just a VPN-locked porn account we *never* let you find. "I'll pwn you all," I snarled—subtlety was def out the porthole now, "I'll chain you to a Cuisinart and make you wear veils. Yeah—fucking Mohammedan *chic*, bitches."

"Somebody's OD'ing on man juice," Duva grinned.

"That dangler is *amped*," Babs nodded.

"Sweet," Cap'n Abba watched me snarfle the air, "he's on the scent. Keelhaul us to port starboard."

"Fucko McSucko," I paced and raved, "I'll smear you skanks into horndog paste—I'll pack your pussies on ice—let me out!" I banged my tin jail cup across those bars like in gangsta noir flicks—and just got more laughs! Sigh—it's true—all us Trickys end as clowns. Sometimes as greasepaint Pierrots with poofy vest buttons, sometimes as slack-tie Rodney Dangerfield slob buffoons. Boys, hang around long enough and you're the joke. "I'll kidnap Irish pixies," I snarled, "I'll start goat fellatio farms, I'll—"

"Thar she blows," Cap'n Abba pointed overdue North—at a gleaming, screaming 90-foot pink moray eel breaching the sky with his fugly mug—and with white flames shooting from his snout. Whoa, who dat? Who else—it's Mobo! Wet scourge of the slimy deep—foaming fiend with rad mad dorsals and a suave attitude—Mobo! A gigantor pink moray eel—way pinker than any upskirt twerk—with teeth that slice night to ribbons. Plus he seethes evil man-juice mojo! Did I mention the white flames? Hah—they're actually fiery jizz—cum napalm! O Mobo—how shall I describe thee? Let me count the waves—now a creamy stew of clotting fire. Mobo makes his own gravy! Mobo's a testo valve that never shuts—and unlike most dudes, he *uses* it. Brutha, he *gets* to be bad—it's written in his contract. Yes, Virginia—there is a moray clause. He's scaled to scale, thick as God's wrist and pwning the seas, muthafucka—who's gonna disagree? Puny girls? He growls at their impotence—he's King Boner! With extra flame sauce. Don't expect romance—there will be no love. No digressions. No pas de drool—the only girlfriend Mobo craves is Chaos. She who cannot be named but just was. Yep—Mobo keeps the bitches *down*.

I *so* want to be him. Plus shhh—Mobo's got a secret. OK, I'll tell you—he's to blame for us dudes—completely. He's our Deus Ex Malum, our frothing font of volatile testosterone—meaning those cum flames! Mobo supplies every broheme on earth with needed spunk—he sprays that male frappé from equator to pole. That's why he's mobbed with sharks that drizzle off him like teething lice. That's why the sea boils with drowned squids when he surfaces. That's why dudes invent sexy head-games in far-off ports—why there's an uptick in murder, hair plugs and logging whenever he swims near. He oozes mega-balls essence—he's a toxic endocrine hydrant! Gush away, Mobo! No doubt he's got a major codpiece market-share and an aftermarket cologne distilled from pure orphan tears. He's what women fear and men dream of being—basically a giant dong. "Hi, girls," Mobo whispers like lava undressing, "wassup?"

"Let's snuff this fucking troll," Cap'n Abba grabs a harpoon, "Ashley—lower the eel boats."

"Aye aye, ma'am," her femme minions tackle the tack. As Mobo swims closer like a live underline, grinning fangs sharper than Inuit wit. "Get 'em, Mobo!" I screech, "smack 'em all! Make them *obey*, mwah ha ha," I sink my own teeth into my perch, gnaw gnaw. Which—duh—just made it easier for Ashley to grab me. "Hook time," she fly-ties me with fishing line around a harpoon tip. "I'll plonk you all," I sputter, "I'll make you keep retard babies to term. I'll mandate pill-box hats," but no use—I'm today's sacrificial hot dog. Squee-eek! "Oink oink, little buddy," Ashley sneers.

"Um, look, baby," I try nice, "you're unfortunately mistaken. I'm sweeter than amnesia—"

"Sucks to lose power," Ashley smiles, "don't it?"

"Sucks to be you," I snarl back, twisting 'til I'm bound even tighter—sigh—as Ashley tosses harpoon-trussed moi into an eel boat, Abba catches me, somebody cusses, the skiff's cut loose and we all plop into steaming grey waves.

31

Water is stupid made liquid—it can't even stay put! Nope, it sloshes around like Satan's bidet, crammed with green crud, teen suicides, plastic zip ties, whale poop—the sea is life's stew. Lukewarm, rancid, and dill pickle extra—no pickle for you! "Hazmat and visors *on*," Abba commands her stupid crew. "Hey dumb cluck," Abba flips down Duva's welding visor, "want to keep that sweet face?"

"No—I mean yes, Cap'n," Duva sulks.

"And?" Abba barks, "everyone. What's next?"

"Stay away from the cum flames," Dora warns.

"Right. And?" Abba demands, "Come on, ladies—"

"Earplugs *in*," Someone else barks.

"Earplugs in," the crew nods.

"Earplugs why?" I puzzle.

"The pink siren," Abba points at el moray, "Dr. Sweet Talk." Who cares—I was as bored as a bald pancake. I mean, sure—I'm headed for certain harpoon-bait death—but what's with all this ship-tack puttering? Cause look, gals—there's Mobo! Introduce me! But no, these chicks are instead yelling 18th-century smack-talk about belaying hardtack and mizzen the astrolabe. 'Til these wet wenches again stacked their hands in a scrum, yelling, "Death to testo!" as Abba got down to snuffing Mobo—and me! Which natch made me wriggle that fishline tighter around my hot-doggy bun. Extra squee-eek! "All is forgiven," I laughed, "OK—I'll do a few dishes. And babysit our brats once a month—"

"If we didn't need you alive, I'd kill you right now," Abba hissed—hah—just like a death-row warden. Next, her crew scuttled around securing this and ballasting that 'til a'ight—we set out to *hunt*, muthafuckas. Where waves and sky smashed into a celestial BLT with me as the sacrificial bacon. But gigantor Mobo didn't snarfle us yet—he just started in with his sweet playah hypno-shtick. He tempts babes with their own estrogen—he's the sugar-rap daddy of us all! He schools us dudes in our luv moves—how to honey-talk after cheating, how to slip inside both a slit and her purse, all while gabbling about our faith and troth and honor—Mobo teaches us the art of *fib*. Plus there's nothing like a spray of salty jizz flames to set the mood. "All you girls comfortable?" Mobo grins like terror, "let's snuggle. I've got a tiny confession—do you remember your pregnant sister?"

"Shut it, motherfucker," Abba sneers, "we can't hear you!

"Some enchanted evening..." Mobo strums the deep with his song, "you may meet a moray..." and fucko, I gotta admit—his voice was sweeter than creamed sleep. He sang like the love child of Fred Astaire and Aqualube—basso profundo and curried soprano drizzled over vocal chords hewn from pink licorice. "You may meet a moray some dayyyyyyy..."

"Still can't hear you, la la la," Cap'n Abba points at her earplugs.

"Will I actually meet a moray?" Ashley beams, as spooked Cap'n Abba stuffs Ashley's loose left earplug back in and hah! Too late—Ashley leaps overboard and swims toward Mobo. "That's right, baby," Mobo whispers, "come to daddy."

"Yes, papa," Ashley squeals, "you still love your Ashley?"

"Like butter loves toast," Mobo circles her, "like sizzle loves sap."

"Ashley—come back!" Cap'n Abba yells, "he lies—he's a fraud!"

"She wants to *separate* us, baby," Mobo hisses, "you gonna let that happen?"

"Ashley!" Abba screams, "remember your fucktard husband?"

"Robert never *really* hit you," Mobo smiles, "it was just a tiny slap—"

"He was nice afterward," Ashley giggles.

"And you gotta admit," Mobo closes in, "you had it coming."

"I did, daddy," Ashley moans, "you were right to correct me."

"And we did it without love," Mobo confuses his message. Yep, he's a guy alright. "Swim closer, baby," Mobo rises, "that's my girl."

"Fucking starboard left!" Cap'n Abba aims but can't throw her Tricky-baited harpoon yet—Ashley's too close to the moray king. While meanwhile, I'm trying to remember everything Mobo says—I mean, come on. Seduction, confusion, dominance, obscure, and allure all in one gigantor pink package? I could *use* some pointers. "Daddy forever?" Ashley smiles.

"Maybe," Mobo rears up, "maybe not," and chomps wet Ashley in half. Whoa! I could hear her femur crunch, her tibia crackle, her veins erode, and skull implode as Mobo chews her to slippery bits. "Yum," Mobo glistens hate and fish lips, "dumb slut pie." Cool! Sorry—I mean ewww—even I'm falling for his hypno-con. And I'm a hard tool to fool. "And you, Abba," Mobo rears, "you shouldn't have left me. You know what happens to bad bitches."

"Still can't hear you—neener neener neener," Abba singsongs and steadies her Tricky harpoon. While I'm still wrestling with wrestle-proof fishline, binding me even tighter to that harpoon's tip. "Remember me as a playah," I groan as Abba aims her Tricky shish kabob.

32

Finally! The arc of history tossed me at an eel. "This is for Ashley," Abba balanced on the fore-stern, "death to the fishiarchy!" and spit-balled me and my harpoon straight for Mobo's noggin. As we whistled through surf and turfy clouds— and struck! Except natch these chicks brought insufficient weaponry—really, skimpy harpoons? For a grievance-clad gigantor moray? As Mobo muttered "Silly," and shook me off like a beau. "That all you got? Pink supremacy!" Mobo screamed and smashed into that eel boat. Where I got a first-row ripple as whew, that wet fishline sloughed off me and I bobbled up in foam-bun grace. Squee-eek! "No fucking way," Abba leapt off her sinking boat, landed on Mobo and stabbed at his gills. Except in the zany mayhem that ensued, she'd lost her earplugs.

"I waited for you—ow," Mobo winced as Stabby McAbba stabbed him, " I kept myself pure, baby—" while snorking a flaming cum stream to show his intent. "You waited for me?" Abba paused her stabbing, "no one else?"

"Only you," Mobo cooed hypnotic blather. "With a heart like a boiled ham—with aching flanks and raking teeth—I waited for only you."

"I know you did," Abba thrilled, "I know. You love your Abba."

"Positively. No one finer—I will follow you..."

"Awww," Abba petted his scaly head. "You sure—no other girlfriends?"

"Aren't you a lesbian?" Mobo sneered—'til Abba just slashed and flashed murder again. While Mobo—who had the upper fin here—breached and sank and rose again in scaly splendor, jizz-torching the last of Abba's eel boats and tipping her crew into the slimy drink. Cap'n Abba went down with that thrashing eel, pinned in its moray fangs, stabbing and cursing—whoa. Hmmm—where'd I see this *obsessed captain vs. evil fish* shtick before—a sea flick with Peter Lorre? Good-fellas? Nah, probably just a Simpsons episode. Lucky for moi, my glued bun—squee-eek, etc.—floated me past that drown-ing, panicked crew—panicking cause of circling sharks. Who chewed those gasping gals into crew chum, shredding Abba's mates into floating spleens and scalps tossed through the air like demonic frisbees. Plus fuckzilla—my turn would be next! Hunger is God's worst snafu—the world's a total chonk-fest ruled by guts and teeth. All hail Prince Colon! Just don't get too close... "Oh look—part of a hot dog!" one shark bitch spotted me—which is natch when Mobo beat her to it and scarfed me down whole.

33

I drowsed like a comet inside a womb—sticky, spit-lit, and churning through darkness. Plus I stank like filthy jaws, ewww—namely Mobo's! Where I was tucked under his tongue. How'd I even stay alive—why didn't he chew me? Who cares—make something up. Explaining stuff's even dumber than watching it. Fuckzilla—what now? Should I floss Mobo's teeth? Howl like Jonah in an ersatz whale? Work on my LinkedIn profile? *I can value-add to any puss-hacking enterprise. I excel at innovation, danger, and peeing.* Was Mobo's belly my true fate—or a mere coincidence, that debutante daughter of chaos? But pondering did zilch as the sea whizzed even louder when Mobo took a dive—eeek! Drowned alive! Lucky I remembered Mr. Dude's frat days.

Meaning when his Sigma-Delta gut got toxic, he'd place a finger down throat and *hurl*, lads. Mr. Frat Dude barfed so much party liquor that his teeth almost morphed into enamel maraschinos. And since the past is mostly a user's manual, I screamed "Bonsai!" and dove for Mobo's tonsils. "Flurk," he hurked me—and instead of sinking into Davy Jones' crawlspace, I floated up into nude light. Now what?

First swim away from breaching Mobo, doofus. But he'd lost interest in snacky moi as he brunched on that all-you-can-eat shark buffet. He chewed those clacky bastards into dorsal gazpacho—whoa. I never heard one scream before.

Now, what else? Oh right, swim to safety. I craved stranding on solid land—but where? Omaha? Poughkeepsie? I know—Seattle! Maybe I could invite Mobo over to chew Wifey Puss to wet splinters. I hate her more every day—hell hath no fury like an unfucked dong. Hmmm—would she go down fighting, or lurk on Mobo's retching tongue? Not to worry—he'd slurp her down like a whining oyster. As I smirked and pictured my twinkling future as a raving male pasha with Mobo as my enforcer. I'd make sullen chicks wear translucent thongs and cougars don bag-cloth and rashes—while my nubile harem ululates a dulcet choral wove from fear and whimsy. I'd be more alpha than any alpha male—I'd thrust and swoon inside fresh puss 'til those pink heavens twinkled with my milky stars. All mouths will seek mine—all breasts will pillow my ennui—spit and teeth will drown my sheath—but maybe not the teeth. For shizzle, I'd make sure Wifey Puss is toast—she'll flee from the male flames splashing out Mobo's mouth —or get toasted to a geezer-quim crisp. No one can defeat King Mobo!

He's taller than air and thicker than a trestle—quick, chain him to that Broadway stage! Taunt him with top hats and cheap playbills—make him roar as iPhones flash and ushers shriek like spanked furies—sell leaky popcorn with a crude Mobo icon—then stand back. As his spooge erupts in flames and finesse, dissolving his chains and all the stage-pit tubas, melting faces and French horns into doom soup—and lets hisself loose on the world! Greasing churches with his milky martini, luring virgins into spread bliss, corralling beta males into filthy drum circles. Maybe you chicks *wanted* this—you *made* it happen—all those stale nights dreaming of improbable boy toys, all those dry-hump thrusts against your George Clooney pillow, all the sniping and griping at whatever dumb dude fell into your Venus twat-trap—your eely avatar doth arise! All hail Prince Mobo—slyer than rayon and wilder than crime. And more handsome than even God's wiener— none of those sky-deity grey hairs on *this* scaley mensch. Never mind the bollocks—here comes the sea dong!

34

Call me Ataxi. Or a bus or Uber or candy-ass red BMW—anything to escape this soggy sea. Where I floated on what's left of my scorched foam-rubber bun. So what goes through your mind, my bruthas, when you're drowning? Pure freaking terror—electrolyte tsunamis that smash your ego into neural wharf-bits as the raving brainstem takes over, screeching escape stratagems that went out with the Dodo. *Get away, get away*! Or not—and usually not—as that cardiac event or head-on crumpling Miata crash or soul-mate's gunplay ruptures you into pools of coroner gunk.

And Mobo? He was a total beached whale! Floating like a pink turd crammed with shark livers and crewmate eyebrows. What good was he to me? This flopping kaiju moray crowned with suckling squid—fucker was even cluckier than them. But who cares what's on Mobo's mind—let him spew fiery jizz for all the brohemes worldwide! Cum is a dish best served mindless—like me, drowning in reverie and brine. And then suddenly—Bonanza! Just like that TV Western except this herd was all dolphins, churning up like aqua Linotype. As those mammals curved near in chariot splendor, glistening like borealis sandpaper and the lead Flipper whinnying under my bloody savior. Meaning who else—Cutie Heart to the rescue, yay! The only organ who would save a gasping dick. "What—glub—are *you*—hack—doing here?" naive me asks.

"Climb on board," Cutie smiled that ultimate femme come-on. So I clambered on her next-door dolphin and pestered her with a gazillion questions, almost two of which made sense. "How'd you find me?"

"I chipped you—feel near your bun top," and for shizzle my nizzle—I felt that teensy GPS chip sewn into my foam garment. "But when—"

"Before you ditched us—I saw you sewing up your dog toy," she reined her dolphin leftwards, the rest of the pod muttering and churning along. "Why does *she* get to rule us?" a porpoise in a toupee asked.

"Don't be heartless, dumb fuck," the lead Flipper snarled.

"I didn't *mean* it," toupee dolphin yelped.

"You planned this all out?" I bugged Cutie Heart. "Yee-ahh!" she spurred her mount, "of course I did. Your adventures are most always tres lethal, boyo—you need a cardiac angel."

"True dat," I didn't argue. Instead—like all dongs—I just seethed inside. Stupid whack organ thinks she knows best... "Oh stop seething," Cutie smiled, "keeping you alive is my job. Yours is to fix Mr. Dude."

"Let's just not return," I cooed, "let's escape. You and me! You could get a job while I lay in a hammock, murmuring your praises—"

"When Mr. Dude's dead, I'm dead," Cutie shushed me, "and you're probably dead too." No way! I ain't been unwell a day since I left—unless you ignore sick with desire, testy with testo, a flaming dildo thrust into nature's hissing slash. What, me die? I'm stronger than ever! I'm the thunder rector that dissolves vectors—the glittering sump in your final id cellar. I flex my veins and love implodes, begging for my sweet healing stick. Besides, us splendiferous dongs never die—we just transform—into memes, court evidence, pagan tchotchkes, gay pastries, whatever.

"Watch your flank," Cutie yelled as a narwhal bumped my mount. "Yikes," I squealed—it was harder staying put than staying sober—getting constantly pre-soaked by those dolphins and their blowhole calliopes didn't help none neither. "Hey, fuck-head," Cutie snarked, "answer me. Do you want us all to die when Mr. Dude croaks?"

"Well, I'm not even sure that I'd—"

"Don't you want me alive?" Cutie brought the herd to bay in a wake-spewing stop. "Or am I too *emo*," she boo-hooed. Probably. But no time to reply—cause here come the waterworks! Tears are the lube in Cutie's luv dynamo—gotta keep those channels *greased*. "You think I'm only good— wah," she sobbed, "good for pumping."

"Depends *what* you're pumping" I kept being a dick. So what—why should I listen to stupid hearts? Every time I get some luv scam ramped up—a fuck buddy who stays pal, a whimsical shag between me and anyone desperate, a running luck streak where all I gotta do is show up—Cutie finds the flaw in the ointment. Got a no-holds boning match? It soon flames into romance twixt my Cutie and hers—eventually ending in gunfire, suicide, or a sterno bender at some Homeless Cardboard Hotel. Finally tease someone down into drooling submission? No way—my De Sade idyll ends up in burning beds, savage 3 a.m. we-gotta-talks, and third-degree public confessions.

"Tricky," Cutie sighed, "you're ranting inside again—I can see it in your—"

"In my flaming eyes? Searing smile? Footwork like a Fred Astaire shaman ?"

"In your budding *length*, hubba hubba" she cooed—and smooched me! "Just" she sighed, "just don't toss me away like yesterday's rubber."

"Some girls *like* being tossed," I smirked. I know, I know, someday I'll pay—but someday's not today.

"Speaking of girls," Cutie shouted over sea spray and porpoise farts, "I had a talk with Wifey Puss. She promised to tone it down."

"That's mighty pink of her. But I can't trust—"

"Tricky, shut up! She is wetter and hotter than ever."

"And she promises not to jail or bore or kill me?"

"No guarantees, you stupid weenie—ain't you learned anything? And who cares what that sullen quim thinks. Let's go save Mr. Bod."

"Hokay."

"Really? You're a prince—wah—" Cutie sobbed. Which got me stiffer than a pirate plank—come on—sobbing? *And* angry? *And* sexy talk? It don't get any better. "We'd better hurry," Cutie spurred her mount, "Mr. Dude's only got a few weeks left before they yank his plug." Hah! Yank.

35

Anyways, we beached in Big Sur, hitchhiked north on the PCH, got jailed, escaped lethal injection—you can't outsmart dumb luck—did a two-day hitch as switchmen at Union Pacific (they were pretty desperate), rode stolen ponies for 400 miles—and ended up back at Mr. Dude's. Who's bod reassembled like a reverse explosion once all his rogue organs returned. I avoided them by hiding in the den—it's bad luck to spot the groom. Especially when he's sneaking away. Which yeah, yeah, I didn't as I perched on a Barcalounger and smoked a stogie big as me. "Tricky," Cutie Heart tweaked her dress hem, "you'd better get dressed."

"Undoubtedly," I stay put and blow smoke rings that look like ice cream lassos. Practice makes parfait.

"Put on your tux, you dodo." Which I smoothly donned cause Cutie H had already shucked my hot-doggy bun off with nail polish remover—why'd I never think of that? Cause I'm a dude. Wait, fucko—my stogie went out. No prob—I quickly zap with a stream of flaming white jizz. "What the fuck?" Cutie yelped.

"I got flame powers, baby—them who meets Mobo get touched with fire."

"Touched is right," Cutie backs up, "are you gonna use that spunk napalm on Ms. Puss?"

"Not a chance," I yawned, "I got morals—"

"And don't forget she's got teeth—" Cutie snarled.

"True dat," I puffed my Havana, "my flame-on is purely protection against Mr. Brain. Let him just try and repress me, mwah ha ha—"

"Wonders and blunders—that's you, boyo," Cutie hugged me. "Hey, Tricky—"

"Hey, what-y."

"Where'd you get that squiggle tattoo?"

"Which what huh?"

"That squiggly tat on your shoulder," she tapped it—where egads! I had the mark of Mobo—same as those Komodos. Cool. "Are you looking forward," Cutie sidled closer, "to banging Wifey Puss?"

"I dunno," I puffed cancer trails, "I don't trust that—er—that vagina."

"But she's *forgiven* you," Cutie pouts, looking redder than sin in her slit Barbie dress.

"Not exactly forgiven," I unfold Wifey P's corny friendship card. "Listen to this. *Dearest Tricky—your moronic ennui-du-mal has nearly snuffed us all. Still, when I'm prone and recalling your evil pheromones, I moan with unease—*

"Oooo, that's rich," Cutie bumped me, "let me see it." So we both plopped on Wifey P's vellum valentine and did a sarcastic read. *When I remember your transgressions—*

"Hah—more like delusions—"

But if all you do is disobey me—

"Oh, you'll obey her alright," Cutie snorted.

"Not fucking likely."

If all the sparrows in all the seas—

"Huh?" I pointed, "sparrow fish?"

"More like muff divers!" Cutie fell off that card—and moi too. As we rolled in whoops smothered in melted guffaws—and you know what that leads to. Perdition? Guilt? Nope—nooky! Must I describe our groovy romp? No doubt—as Cutie gave me an atrial smooch while I stroked her tricuspid clit and we pressed into DNA pixels, me licking her vena cava while her mitral valve pulsed on my veins—'til fibrillating Cutie jumped up. "We'd better stop," Cutie sighed, "better save yourself for the nuptials."

"True," I nod, "Keep the cream hot. I'll ream Wifey Puss like paper. I'll prong her like Medusa's fork, boff her bupkis into slit bliss, I'll—"

"You'll probably forget to put your nads back on," Cutie grinned. She's right—can't wed without the boys. "Vwee-ooo-weet!" I whistled for Bob and Rebob—them's their names—who ran up and howled a doggy sonata. Natch they can't talk—why should they? I do the fibbing for us all with K-tel classics like *Sure I loves you, baby* or *Can't wait to support your five kids* or *That's not porn, it's art*. Want a tip, gals? Just lift my cap—no, seriously—want to groove along with us dongs? *Command* us. Don't repress us, never works for more than a few centuries—command us, make us obey your true booty. Review us stiff troops like Catherine the Great—*Nice sword there, playah. Your cannons are so hard—and those hat feathers are pure Russki Bling. Now get your shizzle and missiles together and muthafucking cap those Romanian thugs. Remember—keep 'em hanging loose—and then get them blown off. My dogs need fresh meat...* Meaning don't be spooked by us dongs—we're as natural as anthrax. Just pin us down with your whimsical wetness.

But don't think on us too much—we sure the hell don't. Just rave and crave us, shove us aside and in. You can't help yourselves without helping us. Life's hard and we're soft 'til your sweet slurp begins. But why the wet obsessions with our spunky tribe? Why hate when you can't wait? Hah—now I get it. It's your filthy, wicked minds—you see dicks everywhere! Lurking on rooftops a la *The Birds*—swarming the beach like dwarf *Jaws* sharks—giggling and darting up your leg with gooey *Aliens* raptor zest—yikes! Here's a clue—Don't listen to us. Most wanks just mumble shit like *Me want sheep* or *Now watch Pornhub pee-pee girls* or *All rabbits are Muslims* or whatever other rabid fluff Mr. Amygdala shoots our way. We're all basically Mr. Caveman—the height of our brackish civilization was fetish masks and human sacrifice. Never trust a prick with a bongo. Or a dick in a tux.

"Tricky," Cutie Heart stamps her teensy foot, "pants *on*."

"Or what?" I grin, sweeping her up in a tango move and dancing us off that armchair. "Hey-yay-yay-yayyy, why do people breaaaaak up," I croon a groovy Al Green tune, "turn around and maaaaake up," I grip a rose petal in my licky tip, "I just can't see-eeeeee—"

"Yooooooou'd never do that to meeeeee," Cutie sings even better than me.

"Alright, baby," I nod, "I'd still rather boff *you*—"

"That was a freebie, son—you can't afford my bloody invoice."

"OK," I grinned, "let's get me hitched."

36

"**H**ere come the nads," every bod part sang, "here come the naaaaaaads—" all perched on that daffodil-strewn bed—Safeway was out of winter roses—and Mr. Dude and Wifey beaming twixt the humid sheets. "Yeah!" Mr. Bladder chimed in, "where's the john?"

"Just follow your nose!" Mr. Brain hisses. Whoa—that grey sucker's gonna blow major artery someday. "Bro," I touched his stem, "just chillax—the best man never steals the show."

"Right. Sorry, sorry."

"Alphonse!" some oozing blob shrieks, "don't apologize!"

"Who's that lump?" Cutie Heart points.

"My date," Mr. Brain beams, "her name is Ms. Tumor."

"Pleased to eat you," Ms. Tumor curtsies. Whoa! Braniac's date is mondo ugly—I can't tell if that's her mouth or her butt crack. Or both. Plus her dress is even fuglier—what's the fabric made from, dead veins? "Yeah, I donated a few," Mr. Brain shrugs.

"Alphonse gives me *anything*," Ms. Tumor grins like a sick virus.

"Um, yeah—that's great," I edge away—this is *not* gonna end well.

"Everyone say cheese," Cutie Heart snaps a group pic with her Hello Kitty iPhone.

"Ain't he gnarly?" Big Brain throws a neural goo loop around my shoulder. Note to self—def keep Blobbo Brain away from surfer slang. "You so *corny*," Wifey's Brain elbows Mr. Brain—wow. Even *those* two made up! Which def ain't gonna last long—good thing, too. I can't *wait* for some tussle-primed booty—anger and wetness are joined at the lip. "Here comes the bride," some organ strikes up the organ as Wifey Puss marches from the closet, all decked out in white panty lace, with Ms. Pancreas and Ms. Appendix holding her train. "Ain't she a beaut?" Cutie beams, "I—I always cry at weddings—"

"You cry at stop signs," I tease her, "you weep during cold-sales calls," 'til Mr. Brain elbows my ribs. "Shhh, brah," he whispers, "Mr. Soul's about to begin." Whoa—they got Mr. Soul to officiate! You hardly *ever* see Mr. Soul—usually he's blind drunk in some chapel alley, babbling about the Nicene Creed or consubfabulation—but that righteous dude was both sober and solemn. "Dearly biological," he drones, "we are gathered here to witness—"

"Witness this, muthafucka!" Wifey Puss yanks her dress off and mwah ha ha—runs at me! A'ight! Nothing finer than eager poon. Unless it's the waft and weave of fireflies strumming their lit butts while swallows chase a nude moon—unless it's memory Polaroids you shake 'til the silver-nitrate dew sizzles into pink truth—through daydream HD flashbacks built from wet pixels that shudder alive—through the Gila-monster dawn where swarming tongues stutter in and out of light—through a crude puppet show made from naxty gestures and raw jokes—hah! I could *feel* Mr. Dude writing again. I want to lick his every whisper, to lap fire and spit gossamer vomit, to— "To maybe pay attention?" Wifey Puss hugs my waist, "to maybe not mutter while your new bride smooches you?"

"You're right," I fib, "what say we sneak away and—"

"And do what's done," Ms. Puss licks my quivering tip and we rush under the bed and—hey—stop spying! Don't you got your own booty to snout out? Then snout it now—grab that brass lass or slut munchkin, nudge her pleats aside and lickity split her dreams into an oral borealis—taste her proud pheromone cloud—savor the quaver as hot love drums the dumb world away. Fuck Fate in the eye and date-rape Death. Lift heaven's hem and rise.

Honokaa – Reykjavik – Port Angeles

Ron **Dakron** is the author of the novels *Tricky, Hello Devilfish!, Mantids, Hammers, Newt,* and *infra*. His work runs the gamut from surrealism to sci-fi pastiche. Born in Chicago, Dakron played in garage bands before moving to Seattle, where he worked as a street violinist and house painter. He instigated various poetry slams with a confrontational style "drenched in faux punkery." Dakron considers himself "a proud working-class novelist who dreams up Big Lit."

www.ingramcontent.com/pod-product-compliance
Lightning Source LLC
Chambersburg PA
CBHW020342260626
47156CB00004B/1645